I0822380

Dead Wrong

Melica Niccole

Hampton Publishing House, LLC

Dead Wrong was published by

Hampton Publishing House, LLC
P.O. Box 29201
Columbus, Ohio 43229

ISBN 979-8-9866655-3-5

Printed in the United States of America

Dead Wrong

Written by
Melica Niccole

Foreword by
Melica Niccole

Cover Designed By
Soulo Theory

Edited by
Charity Martin-King,
Roy Ross
&
Vian Yon

Publishing Company
Hampton Publishing House, LLC

This book is dedicated to my family & best friend. You have been very supportive in my education & writing. It means a lot when I can share my world with you.

-Love you.

Table of Contents

Introduction

I began writing Dead Wrong in April of 2007. It was a very exciting process because it was my first book, and I was so full of energy. During the process of writing the book, I was going to school and working two jobs. Adding an additional task to my schedule surely would not hurt me. I was already working hard, so staying up a couple more hours a night would be ok, especially if it was toward making a dream come true.

When I wrote each night, you could say that I let my imagination run wild to the point that reality took over and said, "I want in on this." I wrote the book with some fictional and non-fictional aspects of life included in it. It was my intention to allow readers to relate to the story, as if it was written about them.

Readers will be able to relate to some of the friendships that take place, advice that is given and violence that is exposed. Life is unpredictable and so are some of the characters in this story; they will have you laughing with enthusiasm, smiling with sincerity, and jumping with anticipation.

I recommend this book for your book clubs, reading groups, and domestic violence prevention programs. At the end of the book, you will find discussion questions, which will assist you with talking about those hard to discuss relationship topics.

Dead Wrong

Remnants of the Past

"You are dead wrong. Dead wrong. I am going to make you pay. Consider yourself dead. You are nothing to me. If I can't have you, then no one can." Those were the words that I heard from my hospital bed. I replayed those words over and over in my mind. I couldn't seem to let go.

The last thing that I saw was a young man drenched in blood, saying "You made me do this to you. How could you? I loved you. You stupid heifer. You make me sick. You're gonna pay for what you've done to me. And believe me, you will pay."

Now, I lay lifeless in a hospital bed because of the man who spoke those words. I guess you could say he was the source of my undoing, vowing to punish me for my indiscretion.

I couldn't believe what happened. He was everything that I yearned for; however, there was something about him that I couldn't place my finger on until we became intimately involved. How could I have done such a thing? I've always considered myself wise and reasonable. Now, it was time for me to own the truth. I was wrong. Dead wrong. I needed to admit it, whether I wanted to or not. He was just the person to teach me how wrong I'd been.

My life had taken a turn for the worse. The situation was out of control. The first question I faced was how? How would I take a situation like this by the reins? There were so many events that had occurred that it felt like life would never return in my body. I was limp from frustration, shock, and deceit.

Ms. Smith

Most of my friends call me Taz. As a child, the name sort of grew on me like fungus on a foot. It was a name that I'd always tried to get rid of but could not. As it was explained to me by my mother, I was whimsical. She said, "People think they have you all figured out, and then, like the Tasmanian devil, you spin out of control, leaving people confused." She was right. As an adult, I learned to live with the Tasmanian Devil syndrome and master my emotions, unless I was upset to the point where rationalization had to be thrown out the window.

My real name is Tasha Marie Smith. I'm 6-foot, skin the color of butterscotch, and body the shape of a Coca-Cola bottle. My hair is naturally curly. I decided to do the natural thing when I was about 20. No more strain, heat, and breakage on this head. It was time for me to find my roots and embrace them. College really changed me. I started to look inside of myself because the campus demonstrations, nasty stares from other races, and just the fact of being black. If I didn't embrace my heritage, how could I expect others to embrace it?

I am from the 'Nati': Cincinnati, Ohio. Most people called it the "Nasty Nati". To me, it was home. I lived there until I was 14. My mother and father decided to move the family to The Capital City: Columbus, Ohio. Ohio was the home of the Buckeyeneers, Columbus Team, Bow Moss, Halle Bush, Ruby Denise, and Roni Morrison.

I am twenty-seven years young, but I look seventeen. People tell me I've been blessed with a youthful look about me. I love looking young because I can wear all types of clothing. I can wear some things that older adults cannot and get compliments on it. The disadvantage about looking young is that I am carded at every club I go. Matter of fact, most of the people I kick it with must be carded. Twenty-seven is great though, because I'm not too young and I'm not too old. I am wonderfully in the middle.

Currently, I attend The Carlton State University. I am obtaining a master's degree in Public Health. I completed my undergraduate work at the Cincinnati University. I chose the Cincinnati University because it allowed me to stay in touch with some of my friends, but when it came time to move on, it was time to move on. You could say that I am very educated and goal-oriented, from what I've been told. I want to maximize my potential, no matter what it takes.

My life is well put together. During the day, I work for the state at the health department as a community health prevention specialist. My job involves devising community health projects toward decreasing health disparities and increasing life expectancy. I've worked for the health department for three years now. I enjoy my job because I am unyielding in the fight against disease. I believe I can make a difference increasing the quality of life for families and communities. What I like most about my job is working with individuals directly and assisting them with accessing resources.

The people are the reason for devising community programs and prevention methods. Clients I serve help me realize how I can be a better professional and how to serve them. I couldn't see myself anywhere else. Maybe, when I get my master's degree, I will advance to the role of supervisor or administrator.

To provide a snapshot on my love life, there isn't much of one to talk about. It's entirely my fault I'm alone. I'm too picky, consumed with my own life, constantly thinking about the future, and did I mention I'm picky? I just want more for myself than some men have to offer. I don't want a partner who is lazy, arrogant, trifling, ignorant, and uneducated. I take my mother's philosophy to heart. She's always saying, "I can do bad all by myself," and she's right. I don't need a man in my life to help me achieve being broke and stressed. That, I can accomplish on my own.

My past relationships have never lasted too long. The longest relationship I have been in lasted for about a year. I was only sixteen. He and I didn't talk often and when we did, we didn't have much to say to each other. He would call and say, "Whatcha doing? I'm on my way over." He was my first, so it was hard to let him go. Not because of our connection to each other, but because the sex was good.

I've grown to be more independent. I want to do things for myself. If I am going to be in a relationship, I want my man to be a carbon copy of me: striving, determined, sexy, educated, and driven. I want my man to uplift me and challenge my mind. Often, my boy friends gain knowledge from me. Just once in my life, I want to gain something from someone else. I need that role model type of man.

I want to take this time and thank the Lord that I don't have any kids. I'm not about to bring a child into this world full of pain, suffering, and selfishness. I must admit that the selfishness is due on my behalf. I'm not ready to share my world with football practice, gymnastics, or any other child-related activity.

Also, I want to get married before I have any children. It's the best thing to do. So, since I'm not dating anyone currently, children are out of the question. My parenting skills wouldn't be the best anyway. Nowadays children are just so disobedient that you would have to abuse them just to keep them in line.

The other day, I saw this woman in the store with her daughter. Her daughter looked as though she was five. Five is an age where a child should have known better. The little girl began to throw a temper tantrum because her mother would not get her a Blue's Cool Doll Baby. The little girl fell out on the floor screaming and kicking. The mother walked over to her daughter, said her name softly, and explained why she couldn't get the doll.

If that had been me, things would have gone a little bit differently. I would have snatched my daughter up off the floor and told her she better get out of my face with all that crying. I would have also said I'll give you something to cry about. My lack of patience is the very reason I don't have children. I don't' want them to turn out like me when I was a child: bad as hell.

My other issue with kids comes from my mother's previous babysitting days. I promise, my mother raised everyone in the whole damn neighborhood, including my cousins. That's here nor there though, I'm just anti-kids right now.

Making Moves

In working towards my master's degree, I knew I needed extra income. It was hard on me: a mortgage, car note, and other bills. I needed money and fast.

One Sunday morning, I glanced through the Employment Section in the newspaper. My eyes skimmed through the paper, finally settling on something that read: *The Flavor in need of a part-time office assistant. Some experience is required; however, willing to train.*

There was something ironic about seeing the ad in the paper. The Flavor was an upscale nightclub in downtown Columbus. I found irony in that because The Flavor was my 'spot'. It's a place I can chillax and kick it. I practically knew all the staff, managers, and regulars. This was a sign; I was destined to work at The Flavor. The position required minimum experience, which was great for me. If any major experience was required, I guess I would be S-O-L.

I searched through my cell phone for J-E's telephone number. Finally, I found it: Jay Evans. Jay had previously given me his number when he needed help with publicizing an event for Mary Jay. He was a nice guy: respectful, honest, and to top it all off, sexy. He made you want to get on your knees and thank the *Lord* for creating such fineness.

I called J-E and his voicemail picked up.

"You have reached J-E's voicemail, please leave me a message. If this is regarding any business transaction, please contact me at 614-259-…."

"J-E, this is your girl, Taz. I was looking at the newspaper today and saw you were hiring for a part-time office assistant. To be honest, I need a little extra cash in my pocket right now and wanted to apply. Please call me back when you have a chance.

J-E called me back in 5 minutes flat.

"Hello?" I answered.

"What's up, Taz? How's everything going?"

For a moment, I got all wrapped up in J-E's deep and mentally stimulating voice that I forgot my reason for calling. "Umm… umm..." Come on girl, think of something fast I told myself. I mean, it's not brain surgery communicating with him.

"Everything is copasetic. I can't complain."

"Umm… is that right?" he said, followed by laughter, which made me feel like one of those dumb chicks. You know, one of those girls who tried to talk about something she had no business talking about, using all those educated words that meant absolutely nothing. I had to get back into character because playing dumb was not one of my strong suits.

"Jay, I was looking in the newspaper and saw you were hiring for a part-time office assistant. I'm interested in the position. What do I have to do to get it?"

"Is that right? Girl, you ain't no beat-around-the-bush type of sista', huh?

"There's no need to beat around the bush. When I want something, I go for it."

J-E's laughter was kind of sly as he responded, "Then why haven't you ever made a move on me, Ms. Taz?"

Thrown off by his response, I responded with quick wit and seduction. "How do you know I haven't tried? Maybe you missed the signals I sent." How obvious does a girl have to be to let a man know she was interested? I glowed every time I saw him. Butterflies made laps in my stomach at the sound of him. Our connection was like a magnetic attraction that made me feel like I had conquered the insurmountable.

"So, Ms. Taz, what signals are those?" he asked, intrigued.

"Expect the unexpected," I said flatly. "So, what's up with that office assistant position?"

After a slight pause, *J-E* responded.

"Are you sure you want that job? You know you will have to succumb to my every desire. Do you think you can handle that?"

I replied, "As long as it is in the job description and it doesn't devalue my character, I'm all yours."

"Oh, we can arrange for you to be all mine. Just let me know the time and date and I'll show you how it's done. Enough about that because we can talk about that later. I think that you would be great for the position. Meet me at The Flavor tomorrow night at 8pm and I can go over some of the details with you. Make sure you're dressed to impress. I want to see all that you have to offer because I already know what you have to offer mentally. You never know, it may get you an early promotion."

Being real with myself, J-E was enticing. He would be just the person to let me expose my wildest fantasies. The good thing about him was that he didn't have a bad reputation like most of the men that worked at The Flavor. I knew it would be a bad choice if I decided to make J-E my goal. We were friends and had been for a couple of years now. I didn't want to mess up our friendship by getting intimately involved. Things could get complicated.

"Thanks J-E, see you tomorrow"

"Sure, thing sweetie. Oh, yea. One more thing..."

"J-E, if you don't stop it," I cooed. "I will be there tomorrow at 8pm, in the attire that I think is appropriate. See you tomorrow, J." I didn't even wait for his response because I knew it would be something about hooking up.

Friday night couldn't come soon enough. My full-time job had done a number on me this week. I was stressed and ready to party. My cell phone registered three missed calls and two voicemails. The first voice message was from my baby sister. "Taz don't forget you are watching Isaiah on Saturday. I'll call you later."

The second message was from J-E.

"Hey baby girl. I wanted to remind you about our meeting tonight at 8pm. I've been waiting for this all week. It'll be great seeing you and hopefully have your fine ass working for me and possibly on top of me. See you soon."

I took a deep breath, as I slumped down on my couch. It was going to be a long weekend. My eyes moved toward the clock on the DVD player. It was already 4pm.

Fatigue moved through my body as I thought about my weekend again. Oh, how my body was so weary. I laid on the couch and stared at the time on the DVD player, while fighting back tiredness. Darkness filled the air, followed by the sound of Luther Vandross's song, "If Only for One Night" quietly playing in the background.

The darkness began to clear as a white cloudy substance filled the air. I glanced down to see a white flowing gown that had some sort of design around the hemline. There was a small breeze that blew and shifted my gown a little toward my calves.

The clouds faded, illuminating a man with his arm interlocked in mine, walking at an unhurried pace. There was a feeling of excitement and joy that embraced my spirit. It was also nervousness. The pictures of the people surrounding me were obscure. Beautiful music faded into the background and a new song began to play. The music was unrecognizable, but it is evident that I liked the tune by the graceful motions that start occurring within my body.

The destination in which my fellow traveler and I had been so accustomed to walking had finally been reached. He disengaged his arm from mine and placed my hand into another hand. The new hand is shaking and somewhat wet. as if it had been dipped into warm water.

The hand pulled me close, folding up a veil that had been covering my face. There was a glare from the sun, which only allowed me to see the silhouette of this person. The sunlight glare revealed a perfectly cut goatee with a light mustache. The person shifted forward, which took away the glare of the sunlight and provided transparency to what stood before me.

I squinted my eyes to take a closer look. The clouds quickly fade into darkness, and I heard a piercing sound…

Sluggishly, I turned off my phone alarm. I glanced to my radio that was playing Jagged

Edge: “Meet me at the alter in your white dress, we ain’t getting no younger, we might as well do it. I feel you are the wild girl I must confess, let’s get married.”

Laying back down on the coach and staring at the ceiling, I breathed out what could have been and then glanced at the DVD player. I dashed to the bathroom in an attempt to regain some of the time I lost. I needed a shower and quick.

It took me seconds to strip down and jump into some refreshingly warm water. Oh, how good it felt. Each small droplet from the showerhead hit every inch of my body. I positioned my face in the pathway of the water to cleanse it. A warm sensation filled my body, sending chronic currents down my spine and to my nerve-endings. Breathing became heavy and sporadic. The feeling was sensational.

I jumped out of the shower and headed to my bedroom closet. My closet was full of clothing; some for partying and some professional. My eyes frantically searched to find an outfit. I finally found it. The outfit was sexy and at the same time professional.

Moisturizing my body helped with keeping my skin smooth and lovely. The underwear set I chose was made of black silk. I chose a form fitting bra for the occasion to give me an extra lift. The lift took me out of a committee I was a life member of; *The-Itty-Bitty-Titty-Committee*. My panties gave me a natural curviness that added to my figure.

After slipping on my undergarments, you know I had to indulge in my cola figure. Just as I suspected; dyme piece material. My mind started to reminisce on that song by *Jamie Fox* and *Adena Howard*, *"I got my T-shirt and my panties on."* That was my jam.

I hate to be narcissistic, however my body was tight. I was a size 6, tall, and thick. Everything was in the right place and blossoming. My chest and butt were not too big; they were the perfect size for my body type.

I put my pants on next. At my dismay, they didn't slip right on. Size 6 was the correct size; however, it was a struggle getting them over my butt. Why can't mainstream stores carry jeans to fit the natural curviness of women with hips?

Next, I found a light blue belt to go with my blouse. I lived to coordinate my attire and life. As I slipped on my blouse with a slight tug of the corners, an hourglass figure was exposed. Damn girl, you are going to turn heads tonight!

I had to rock some 'killa' shoes with my hot outfit. I knew just what to wear; 3" heels. The straps connected right across the middle portion of the toes, straight up the middle portion of the foot, and around the ankles. Small diamond chips emitted bright rays of color from the straps as movement occurred.

I took on some of the characteristics of the shoe. My walk was very distinct. Confidence overflowed within my blood stream causing my hands to swayback and forth. My hips rotated on my pelvis, which gave the men something extra to think about.

My hair was the next task to complete. I kept it well conditioned and groomed. My beautician was the best there was in the whole world. Latisha Baxter was a great beautician. She was the best that there was, not just because she was a hair dyin', hair stylin', hair crimpin' magician, but also because she was my baby sister. Tisha did my hair every other week at the "*Family discounted rate*." You got to love those family discounts. They come in handy every now and then.

All I had to do was to be available to watch my nephew *Isaiah* whenever *Tisha* needed me. *Tisha* always let me know a few days in advance, so I could prepare. Although I hated children, I couldn't give up watching him because he was my *Mini-Me*. He reminded me of myself when I was younger; hyper, honest, and bad. He was always into things, told people how he felt, and sometimes needed a reality check.

A Golden Hot flat iron was what I pulled from my closet. I decided that I would go with the straight look. My hair was so thick that I needed the flat iron to thin it out. Straightening my hair took about 30-45 minutes. It was now 7:10pm. Intuitively, I needed a good hour and a half to get ready because perfection took time, and I was the keeper of it.

After my hair was finished, I put on a suit jacket. One more glance in the mirror. My outfit would not go unnoticed tonight. I walked out of the house with a conceited *Sas'*.

My garage door opened slowly as I started my 2008 *Chevrolet Impala SS*. My baby was fully loaded. It had a CD player, automatic windows, air bags, seat belt detector, seat warmers, and sunroof. It was all black with tinted windows. I named it after the most distinguished man in the world. He was sexy with a nice frame, enticing, and just stunning. Yes ladies, I named my ride *Morris*. When I rode in *Morris*, he made me quiver with excitement and adrenaline flowed rampantly within my body produced by his ability to speed. He was what I yearned for, even if it was a figment of my own imagination.

The Flavor parking lot was vacant. My sunglasses sat stationary on my face as I parked near the entrance. The wind blew straight through my hair.

I entered the club, glancing to my left, then right. The staff was setting up for the influx of patrons that night. People were mopping floors, wiping tables, and setting the mood. I couldn't believe I was a step closer to working at The Flavor. This wasn't a dream come true or anything. It was simply shocking that I would work at my favorite night club in Columbus. I was thrilled at the opportunity.

I went straight to the bathroom. The lightening in the bathroom was dim and mellow and went well with the calm lilac wall colors. There were fresh lilacs on the sink. On the right of the sink was a small table that consisted of a jar, lotion, mints, and towels.

Two-dollar bills lie lonely in the spacious jar on the table. There were three mirrors on the wall: the front wall of the sink, and the left and right side of the sink. Soft music circulated throughout the bathroom. This music made the bathroom experience pleasant. "If *this world was mine*" played. This must have been a *Luther* night.

First thing, I washed my hands. After washing my hands, I proceeded to smooth out my hair. I retrieved a small black comb from my purse. I combed my hair back in place and went on adjusting my clothing.

I had to be sure everything was put back into place when I went to see J-E. He was a fine, fine, 'F'ine brotha'. I wanted him to always see me at my best or as close to it as I could get. I finished up with fixing my clothing, so now it was time to see the man of the hour.

As I exited the bathroom and made my way past the bar, two of three bartenders smiled at me. I smiled right back.

The Flavor attracted many people. People would come to the club in dresses, suits, and nice professional attire. Sometimes, you encountered an individual who wore sunglasses in the club, drank champagne, and was fashionably savvy. They were definitely 'doing them.'

The whole set up of the club was very nice. On the first floor were two bars, a bathroom, dance floor, and a pool table. The Flavor was immaculate. It could fit a whole shipment of cars in it.

The first bar was near the entrance. It attracted people as soon as they entered the club. Near the dance floor, toward the wall, are stairs. The stairs led to the upper level, which most of my friends called "The Upper room." The second bar sat in a back corner. The pool table was adjacent to the second bar in a small room.

On the second floor was the V.I.P section. This was where it all went down. If your reputation had any type of credibility, then you were what was known as a "Flav-In."

J-E's office was on the second floor. His office door remained closed most of the time, although he may occupy it. J-E mingled with the guests from time to time.

As I reached the last step to the V.I.P section, I was surprised to see J-E sitting in the lounge. He was enjoying a drink, which looked like X-rated. He was clean-cut and looking sexy. The platinum hair cut he wore complemented his head and made me want to run my hands through it.

I looked him from head to toe; admiring the way his crisp white shirt sat firmly against his body. Imaginations started to spark my mind about the way he filled his black slacks as he got up to embrace my wanting spirit.

I had to admit, this man had swag. He wasn't the type that looked down on others for lacking sex appeal. He was the type that acknowledged people's other characteristics and embraced them. J-E had an aura about him that mesmerized the whole room.

His perfectly cut body sat upright in the cushioned chair as he held his drink in his right hand. His eyes were closed as his thumb and middle finger rubbed his temples. Although he seemed tense, it didn't seem to deter my mind from fantasizing about him. Fantasizing about his nice body up against mine, giving into every desire I could conjure up. What a night that would be? There were a few questions I pondered. Could he handle me? Could he handle a woman who would put love into everything she did? Could he handle letting down his guard down about the assumptions of men and women and just fall in love for what it was and not for what it should be?

Reality brought me back from fantasy world. I walked straight over to J-E. “Hey, handsome, what it do?”

J-E instantly stood up. He stroked my back and said “Magnificent! Now that Daddy’s Girl made her way back home.” J-E had always referred to me as ‘Daddy’s Little Girl’ or ‘Baby Girl’, since we first met.

His words made me tremble with excitement as he touched me and whispered in my ear. We both sat down. His eyes seemed to glow. “So, Baby Girl, how have you been doing?”

“I’ve been fine,” I said with a deep sigh of satisfaction. I wanted to say, “Thinking about you,” but I couldn’t mustard up the words.

His next words made me want him even more when he said, “That you are.” I smiled at him. I was at a loss for words.

I think he could tell I was nervous. He broke the ice, “The job description says that I’m looking for an office assistant. In knowing where your experience lies, I know you are very reliable and responsible. The days are Thursdays, Fridays, Saturdays, and some Sundays for about 20-25 hours a week. The pay may not be what you expected; however, it’s all I can do for right now. It’s ten dollars an hour.”

I was ready to accept. The position sounded great. There weren’t many part-time jobs that I had seen willing to pay ten dollars an hour. I listened to him as he continued to explain the job description and perks.

"In assisting me with the office responsibilities, you would update information, make copies, fax, receive and make calls, assist with monthly budgeting for profits and expenditures, and any other office work that may need to be completed. The benefits of working here will be free admission with a guest list up to 5 people, and half price on drinks on certain nights. So, what are your thoughts about the position?"

"Sounds great. When do I start?"

His smile was genuine when he said, "I knew I could count on you. Welcome to the team."

The Flavor

The first people J-E introduced me to were the female bartenders. He told me that it was a great idea to talk to them because they looked out for each other. He introduced them as the delicate flavors of The Flavor.

“The first flavor is Mocha Sensation. Her personality is strong, erotic, and enduring.”

“What’s happening, mama?” she said as she shook my hand fervently and with admiration.

“The next flavor of the night is Vanilla Wonder. She is calm, relaxing, and sometimes viewed as condescending.”

Ms. Wonder spoke up immediately.

“That’s first impressions for you. You’ll see me for who I am in due time. Nice at times, sweet even more, been called a bitch a few times, but bet you've heard it even more." She spoke like a true woman of her word.

"Cinnamon Spice {CS} is the next flavor" J-E said with a smile. "She's a very happy being, funny, and invigorating."

"Hey, Beautiful" she said as she embraced me into her arms and gave me a hug. She made me feel as though we had known each other for years.

"Our last but not least flavor is Chocolate and Vanilla Swirl."

C&V Swirl threw up her hand and looked away.

In seeing C&V Swirl act in a displeasing manner to me, CS said, "Don't mind her. She acts like that to everyone in the beginning. Just be yourself and don't let her get to you. That's all you can do."

"Thanks for the pointers, ladies. My name is Tasha, but you can call me Taz. I'll be working very closely with Mr. Jay Evans as his part-time Office Assistant. If there is anything I can do, please don't hesitate to ask. I'll try my best to assist you, as you are willing to assist me."

All the flavor girls smiled, except for you-know-who. She looked at me in disgust and walked away. The look was all too familiar.

C&V Swirl stood a little too close to J-E for comfort. I noticed that as he spoke, she gazed into his eyes. I even caught her, a time or two, smiling childishly as he said her name. What a loser she was to fantasize over someone who was predestined to be mine. It was the truth, but I guess that's the way life happens. People always fall for those who never think twice about them.

I bet J-E didn't even notice she was wearing a low cut, sleeveless shirt. He probably didn't even see her perfectly styled hair and nails.

"Hey J-E, I see you have a fan club up in here. Boy, you must have that good, good, because it is tryout season up in here; everyone's trying to make the cut."

Laughing lightly, he replied, "Baby Girl, what are you talking about? The only person I want on my team is you. Girl, you wearing my favorite fragrance. *Alluring*, right?"

“I guess you filter out those things you want to and acknowledge the others.” I stared at him amused.

He grinned at me and gave me a slight shove. C&V Swirl stared at us furiously. She had to know that J-E was out of her league. Matter of fact, he was in a league of his own.

The staff was working hard to get everything together to open the doors by 10:30 pm. J-E told me that it would be a week or so before I started. I was fine with that because this weekend was going to be hectic anyways. I needed time to release.

My two best friends, Monique and Coli, called me on my cell phone. I met these young women at *Cincinnati University*. We all had different personalities, but for some reason we got along.

Coli seemed like the introverted type. She got along with most crowds, but she was always portrayed as timid. She wasn't timid though; she just didn't know what to say to people. She was similar to me. She was very social and made good first impressions. Most of the time she was happy because she spoke her mind 99% of the time. She spoke her mind at times when you didn't want to hear it. The difference between Coli and me was that she knew when to shut up. Sometimes, I got on a roll, not realizing who was around me. You know how sometimes you talk about somebody, not realizing that someone around you know them? I really didn't care. However, I didn't need them dissecting and misinterpreting the words I said. I just wished people would tell it like I told it. That's all they had to do. I just wanted to say, please don't confuse my words, please. See, what did I tell you? On a roll.

Now Mo', she was in a class all by herself. She was more of the black power type; militant and ready for war. Every time something happened, she got defensive. Her instructor gave her a C on an exam: "I got a mutha fucking C because I'm black huh?" Her ex-boyfriend married an African: "I guess I wasn't black enough." Her mother asked her if she knew where her purse was: "Are you saying I took your purse? How are you going to accuse me of something like that?" Mo's attitude was ok on some occasions. However, on other occasions, it got on your damn nerves. Sometimes, Coli and I wanted to say “Mo’, if you don’t shut the hell up.”

“Whatcha doing, Taz? You know this is girl’s night out, right?” Mo’ yelled as loud music blared.

“Ms. Taz, what’s going on tonight?” Coli chimed in after Mo.

“Ladies, I’m relaxing at our spot.”

“What!” Mo’ blared without trying to hear me. “You slick trick. You’re trying to get all the men for yourself. We got your number.”

“Mo’, there you go again with all your ranting and raving. That’s the very reason Coli and I do things without you. We’re not trying to hear your I-hate-the-world-tall-tales for not catering to your needs. Do us a favor and grow the hell up."

"Whatever trick, just get to it with the reason why you are at *The Flavor* without us," *Mo'* said bitterly.

Coli laughed.

"Taz, what's going on at The Flavor? I know you wouldn't go out without us. Something special must be going on," Coli said.

That's why I loved Coli. Before she reacted, she got all the information first, unlike Mo'. I think Mo' liked to hear herself speak, so she spoke anytime she had a chance.

"I had an interview with the man of the hour, Mr. Jay Evans. He was looking oh-so-fine. We flirted like always, which made me want him even more."

"Interview! What for?" Mo' blurted out. She could get on my nerves sometimes and I think this was the night she would get on mine. I think I had psychic powers because I promise I saw her future. Everything was becoming oh, so clear. I could see a beat down in her near future. The afflicter looked similar to me. You know what? I think it was me. She only had to do one thing to divert my vision and that was shutting up sometimes. That's all she had to do. I knew, even she could do that.

"Well, since you asked so nicely, Mo'. J-E was looking for a part-time office assistant. I thought it would be a great opportunity, so I applied. I start in a week or two."

Coli spoke to me, very motherly. "Are you going to be ok working two jobs? I know it's a money factor, but you must think about your health first."

"Yeah. I'll be ok. You know I'm a workaholic. This is something I must do. These are my wonder years. I don't get too many of those, so better do it before they are gone."

"Yeah, before you get old, cranky, and bitter like me," Mo' said.

"Lord knows I'm not ready to be the second Wicked Witch of Columbus yet."

Everyone laughed. I think deep down inside, we knew the truth. Mo' tried to defend herself, but it didn't work.

"Well, if you are ok with it, I am too. Alright now, sista girl, what's up with the perks? I know Mo and I are getting in free right?" Coli said eagerly.

“Flava, we taking over,” Mo’ said.

There she goes with all that taking over crap. You had to admit though, it came at the right time. Her words had less of a negative affect if they came at the right time.

“So, ladies, if you would kindly put on your finest dresses and make your way to The Flavor because it’s going down tonight.”

“Ok Taz. We’ll be there about 11:30. Put us on the guest list”

“Ok, I’ll see what my sexiness can do with Mr. J-E.”

Back to Reality

Visitors poured into my hospital room like the opening of a brand-new outlet shopping center. The first people I saw were Coli and Mo'. They were asleep next to my bedside. Coli's hair was out of place, which wasn't like her. She did not leave the house unless her hair was done, clothes in style, and nails on point.

"You made me do this to you. How could you? I loved you. You stupid heifer. You make me sick. You must pay now for what you have done to me. And believe me, you will pay." For some reason, my throat was sore. Matter of fact, my whole body was sore. My right eye would not open. I couldn't seem to move any part of my body either. Oh, *God*! I thought. Was I paralyzed?

The next people that entered my room were my mother and father. My mother walked over to me. She looked very sad and hurt. She looked at me dead in the eye and then motioned to my father. "Go get the nurse."

At that very moment, Mo' and Coli were on their feet. I knew it must be all bad for Mo' to be in a hospital. She didn't like hospitals ever since her niece died in one. Her vow was to never go into a hospital again unless it was life-threatening. Was this life-threatening?

"Taz, sweetheart, we are here for you," my mother said sincerely.

Coli and Mo' grabbed my right hand. They held it so tight that I thought I would die from pain before anything else.

Was I dying? I voiced internally. Why was everyone behaving strangely? Was this my last day on earth? Why couldn't I talk? All these things crossed my mind as my family and friends gathered around me. I think I exhausted myself to the point where I felt a sudden tiredness run across me. I closed my eye to rest.

My eye opened to a new set of people surrounding me. My baby sister was there with her husband and my nephew. There was also a face I hadn't seen in a minute. Kenneth Jenkins; my ex.

My nephew smiled and said, "Mommy, Mommy, look. Auntie Taz, look." Tisha sprung to her feet and said, "Taz, please let us know you're ok. We're all worried, please say something. We love you and want you back at home. Taz, I'm sorry for anything that I've done to you, even as a child. I love you."

A tear filled my eye. Why did my sister speak those words to me? Why could I not speak? Oh, *Lord*! Please give me a sign. Help me to understand why I'm in this predicament.

Kenneth approached my sister. He whispered something in her ear. Next thing I knew, she left the room with her husband and son. Kenneth closed the door and sat next to me on the bed. He placed my right hand into his and began rubbing it.

"Hey, Beautiful. It's been way too long." He spoke with conviction.

"If you wanted to see me, all you had to do was call me. Promise me you'll never contact me like this again."

I could feel the old feelings resurfacing like a wrecked ship washing upon a seashore. *Soft violins streamed from a thin pale man with glasses on. Rose pedals adorned the floor providing vibrant and upbeat colors. The scene was romantic and sweet. It was our first date.* I sat across from a man who spoke with his eyes and examined with his hands. The smile that was permanently imprinted on my face was like no other. It was a smile of security, warmth, acceptance, and unselfishness. It was a smile of love.

A feeling of guilt entered my soul, which released landfills of tears. "Hey, now. Don't do that. It's not your fault we're not together. I look at the break-up as a way for me to come back to you. You've truly been the only woman that I ever cared for and loved unconditionally. I'm still in love with you and I want you to be mine."

The tears were unstoppable now. I let a good man go because I wanted more. He was the best boyfriend I've ever had. He was open with me, showed me love unconditionally, vowed to be loyal to me, and supported all my ideas.

As *Kenneth* continued to show me love and support, there was a soft knock at the door.

"Come in," Kenneth said.

The door opened and in walked a tall, well-distinguished man in a blue collared shirt and black slacks. I squinted to make out the features of this man. He came closer. It was J-E.

J-E began to smile ear to ear. He moved over to the bed and picked up my hand. Kenneth looked confused and then made his way out the room.

"Baby, I've missed you." He gave me a long, sweet kiss on the lips. I couldn't even appreciate his passionate kiss. How could he kiss me so passionately and I couldn't return it?

"I need you to get better, so you can come and live with me," J-E said as he laid next to me with his chin planted on my shoulder. He looked up at me as a lonely tear streamed down his cheek.

"Baby girl, I'm in love with you. I didn't realize it until you weren't around for me to talk to, to bug, or to love. I wrote you a poem to let you know how I feel about you. Here it goes..."

Love…
The feeling that I cannot just hide inside
For if I do
It just eats me alive
Flesh eating parasite
That has no remorse
Don't know where it comes from
But, I know its source
It terrorizes me
Because it just wants to be free
To tell the world
Come hither and see
How true love should be
I cannot live here knowing
Where my life should be going
Without you by my side
My woman
My girl
My do or die

Damn, what a way to tell a girl you're in love with her. Telling me that only made me mad at myself for whatever I had done to get there.

My mind started to recall a few more pictures of what happened to me. I saw a tall slender silhouette towering over me. The person held something in his or her hand. I couldn't make out the object, but a thick dark substance dripped from the end of it. I grasped for air. I was dying.

Mr. Jacob Andrews

It was ladies' night at The Flavor. Everyone was out and about and looking good. It had been 4 months since I started working there. Everything was going well. Everyone respected me and I finally got C&V Swirl to communicate with me.

"What's up, Taz?"

"Hey girl," I responded.

We became closer when I defended her from an unruly customer who got out of control. I stepped in between them when nasty stares and words were traded and led the customer straight to the door with the assistance of security. At first, there was an unspoken sign of respect, which later led to verbal conversations.

C&V Swirl had to realize by now that what J-E and I had were only flirtatious attempts to make our lives full of fun.

I had to work on Ladies Night, but I still made out a guest list. At least my girls could enjoy the night. I knew Mo' and Coli would be down. They went to every event that the club ever held, or it seemed like it. My crew was always in the mood to find a nice man that they could have fun with. My sister wanted V.I.P. status also, so I hooked her up.

I could tell tonight would be my night. It was time for me to meet a special man to help me enjoy life. I needed a change in my life, even if it was a small change.

J-E flirted with me all night, whispering in my ear, touching my neck, and even smelling me. It was the type of night that we could just relax in the beginning before the work began to pour into the office.

"Come on, Baby Girl. Let's dance!" J-E said as he pulled me onto the dance floor. My dress pants, tight-fitting silk shirt, and short-heeled shoes set me apart from the rest of the young ladies. The dress code at The Flavor was dressy; however, you could tell that I was classy and a notch above the rest.

As J-E pulled me onto the dance floor, I glanced over to this gentleman who had been staring at me for the past hour. His eyes followed my every movement. I laid my head on Jay's shoulders and told him about my secret admirer.

"Don't look. There's a guy at the table to the right. He's been staring for the past hour now. It's making me a little uncomfortable."

J-E turned instantly and looked in his direction.

"Didn't I say don't look?"

"I'm just protecting my product."

"Your product," I said with attitude.

With a laugh he said, "Yes, my product. Do you have a problem with that?"

"Yes, I'm nobody's product."

"Feisty, just the way I like them."

We both broke out in laughter and continued to dance. One of the bouncers came over to J-E and told him he was needed for an altercation. They left me standing on the dance floor looking lonely. What a bunch of gentlemen.

In the attempt to not look like a recluse, I moved swiftly off the floor.

Before I could make it completely off, I was met by the most beautiful eyes I'd ever seen. The eyes exuded confidence, strength, sincerity, and looked at me as if they knew me. I was speechless. The man with the beautiful eyes finally spoke.

"Would you like to dance with me, Taz?"

How did he know my name? Did my nonverbal communication unconsciously open my mouth and slip him my name? I thought about his question for a moment because I was usually a people-watcher. I really felt compelled to dance with this sexy man though.

"Yes," I said.

He held out his hand to accept mine within his. It was like we were on the dance floor by ourselves because I really couldn't remember walking past the crowd spaced so sporadically around us. My heart sped up, anticipating any word that hummed from his throat, rolled on his tongue, and slipped through his teeth. All of a sudden, my brain stopped sending signals to my nerve endings. My palms started to sweat, and my arms wouldn't move. My feet felt like a 2-ton truck that had been concreted in the middle of the dance floor to be made a spectacle out of.

He pulled me closer without any resistance. His scent was so powerful that my mind couldn't comprehend the concept. The aroma made me slip deeper and deeper into it with every whiff. The scent was pleasantly enduring.

He whispered softly into my ear. “My name is Jacob. I’ve had my eye on you for a while now. Your soul glows like a golden moon graced by your eyes, which sparkle like 2 stars using Morse Code to radiate your smile. Your body feels like a cup of hot chocolate on a snowy day, which satisfies my ever-wanting need. Your skin feels like a tantalizing dove, which has spell bounded my heart and won’t let go. My soul, my life yearns to be eternally connected to yours.”

“Wow.”

His introduction pierced my soul like a stray bullet abruptly zipping through a crowd of people with a locked target for my psyche. It came from nowhere.

"Did I come off too strong?"

Hell yes, he came off strong. His introduction was stronger than a cup of black coffee with no additives. My mind said yes but my mouth said, "No." Our eyes made a connection, and my mountain-high wall began to crumble as his words hit my ears and turned them into spoken emotions.

He threw me off-guard because I was expecting a thug in a suit to try and spit game. I was expecting, yo shatwy, what's good? Can we kick it or what? You could tell this brotha' read me like a book because I wasn't turned on by the hey shawty, can I get your number type of man. I was a woman who needed a man to approach her and make the connection of feeling wanted and respected. He did all of that in less than 5 minutes.

"Impressive introduction."

"Only the best for the best."

"Is that right?"

"Yep."

"So do you come here a lot?"

"Yes, ma'am."

"Why haven't I seen you then?"

"Probably because you weren't looking for me. I've always seen you and you've always caught my eye. What does a brotha' have to do to get to know you?"

This brotha' didn't waste any time trying to get the digits. I had to respect his straightforward hussle. I didn't like people beating around the bush no ways.

"First of all, you got to be on my level. Right now, I'm not looking for love. Just someone who can stimulate my mind. I want a friend who can encourage me and give me inspiration. I'm tired of giving others inspiration. I need some of my own."

For a minute, I thought I turned him all the way off. In the past, when I did my *Inspiration Speech*, men walked away. I expected him to do the same.

I was very surprised at his reaction. "Is that all?"

"No, that's not all. I'm just waiting for you to turn and walk away."

"Why would I do that?"

"Because others have done that when I started my Inspiration Speech."

"I'm not like others. I know women need to be love and feel inspired. As men, we must realize that women have needs as well. In owning the truth, I understand exactly what you mean."

Damn, where had this man been all my life? I didn't want to look as if I was taken by his words; a hopeless romantic who fell in love with every man who was good with his words. His intentions were unclear, so I paced myself.

Jacob and I sat in the corner and had a nice conversation for about an hour or so. We talked about life, our families, and even love. I know, I know. It was too early to talk about love, but our connection was out of this world.

I looked into his pretty green eyes and saw something I tried to push back into my mind. My imagination started to take flight. Things I had no business thinking about surfaced. I saw two naked bodies connecting with each other so intensely. The bodies moved rhythmically in tune with each other. My body cringed as I felt a thrust inside of me.

"Are you ok?"

"Umm…I'm cool."

I guess my cringe wasn't an imagination. I had to keep my composure. Lord knows I should keep my thoughts under wraps, for I may scare him off.

J-E walked up and interrupted an in-depth conversation. There was a look of jealousy that swept its way onto his face and made its way into his throat.

"Taz, I've been looking for you everywhere. You need to get to work. I'm not paying you to socialize."

What crawled up his ass? He'd never talked to me like that before. I wasn't going to take his macho form of discipline. He had to respect me.

Jacob's facial expression went from relaxed to uptight.

"Taz, are you cool?" Jacob said.

"Duty calls."

Stares as if they were defending their turf were exchanged between J-E and Jacob.

The resistance between J-E and me was intense. An uncomfortable feeling was in the air and did not dissolve with silence. We both were stubborn and did not like to admit our wrongness.

"Taz, the way I approached you tonight…"

"You're forgiven."

"WHAT? I didn't apologize."

"No need. I know you are sorry because you approached me sort of foul."

"The foulness wasn't directed toward you. It was directed toward the guy trying to get to know you by feeding you with lies. I expressed it toward you, but it wasn't meant for you."

"J-E, he was a cool dude. He was down to earth and very open."

"That tells you right there, something's up. Anytime a dude is down to earth and open on the first meeting, you need to do your research. Guys get a sense about a woman by the way she walks, talks, smells, and looks. They can tell you everything you want to hear by what they have observed in you. He's probably a stalker, especially if he calls you within the first three days."

"Do I detect jealousy in the room?" Could this be true?

He laughed and said softly, "Not jealous, but concerned." Our conversation ended there because we had work to do.

There was so much work that going back downstairs wasn't an option. When I finally made it back downstairs, it was 3:30am. The

Flavor was closed for business. J-E walked me to my car, gave me a big hug, and told me to call him when I made it home.

What was I going to do about Mr. Jacob? He seemed sincere and I loved talking to him. I had to get to know him somehow. Hopefully, he would call.

So, We Meet Again

It had been nearly a good two months since I met Jacob. I wondered if I would ever see him again. Obviously, he made a great impression on me. I couldn't stop thinking about him. For some reason, though, I made myself put the whole encounter behind me. What did I really know about this man anyways? We had only talked once.

My thoughts of him cleared as I got dressed. It was Friday night, and I didn't have to work. I know you're wondering, "How did she manage that?" Well, all I did was go straight up to J-E and tell him I wasn't working tonight. My words did not come out exactly like that, but close. They came out *more* like, "J-E. Baby, Honey. I need Friday off. The girls want to kick it.

He laughed and said, “Sure, because you’ll end up here anyways.” Sad, but you know what? He was right because that was where we ended up.

When J-E saw me, he laughed. His eyes surveyed my body, looking me from head to toe.

“Damn, girl, what do I have to do for you to wear something like this for me?”

Ok, maybe my outfit was a little revealing, but short, tight, and low-cut was my style.

“J-E, you should be more worried about getting me out of something like this instead of wearing it.”

His eyes got wide with excitement. He moved closer to me and whispered, “I see this little red number has you extremely confident, but that’s good. I like my women confident and experienced. I know you're all the above, so let's get it. Red bone, you follow the yellow brick road right up to Big Daddy's office and I can show you just how the big bad wolf can get this little red dress right off you. And that's real."

His facial expression didn't show any signs of smirking. All the words he spoke were real. I could see the desire in his eyes.

J-E grabbed my hands and excused us from the others. He led me onto the dance floor. "*Ima make it do what it do*" blared from the speakers. He held me close, touching every inch of my body. It felt so right to be with him.

J-E placed his mouth near my shoulder. "Baby, if you were mine, I would treat you so good. You're everything I need in my life. I won't stop until you're mine." His words moved through my ear, right to my hips. I wanted to say yes so much, but I knew he was already involved.

I enjoyed the moment and didn't say anything. The mood was so right. His hands moved further and further up my back until he was touching skin. I finally got the urge to say something. "J, baby. Slow down. Let's not move too fast. I know you're taken and I'm not trying to mess that up." He looked at me. His eyes spoke a language of *let's get it on*, while licking his lips and rubbing his chin.

I didn't even let him defend himself before speaking again. "I'm not looking for any jealous woman to challenge me for what's already her's. Sexy yes, drama no. If I was a woman that didn't mind, I would be all over you.

I'm not looking for that though." I walked off the dance floor to the bar, next to Mo' and Coli.

"Damn, Taz, you have skills, girl." Mo' said as she handed me a drink. Coli was like, "Yeah, that's called the lady in red skills."

Mo' pointed out that *J-E* was still staring at me from the dance floor, where I left him. After a few minutes, he disappeared. I felt bad because I really liked J-E, but I couldn't get my hopes up for nothing. He was probably drinking and let the alcohol do the talking. Now that I think about it, alcohol makes you tell the truth. I should have jumped all over him like a sack of deliciously sweet peaches, bur really that wasn't my steelo.

The next thing I knew, someone was tapping me on my shoulder. I just knew it was J-

E, so I turned around saying "I knew you couldn't get enough of...."

I was pleasantly surprised by another face, Jacob. "Hey, Sexy Mama. How you been?"

I smiled. "Hey."

I was trying to keep my cool, even though my smile gave away my anticipation.

"It's been like years since I saw you," I said sarcastically.

Mo' and Coli looked confused. Jacob saw their confusion and said, "I'm sorry, where are my manners? I'm Jacob. You must be *Tasha's* friends?"

Mo' then blurted out "Ohhhh, so you're Jacob?"

I could have truly smacked that chick. I didn't want him to know that I'd been talking about him already. She chose this one time in life not to be the introverted person people thought her to be. I threw Mo' a look that could have scalded her unborn child.

Coli shook her head in disbelief.

"Come on, Mo', let's go see what's going on upstairs." I shot Coli a thank you look and returned my attention to Jacob.

"So, I guess I made a good first impression seeing that your girls know about me already."

I laughed and said, "I barely even remember you, what is your name again?"

"Cute. Real cute." He moved closer to me.

We decided to grab a drink from the bar and then relax in the corner while chatting. I had to say, he looked GOOD! He was dressed in all black. The top button of his shirt was undone, exposing a portion of his chest. His cologne even smelled good. The scent smelled similar to *Trajectory*. *Trajectory* always sent me into a tantalizing sniffing ecstasy trying to inhale the whole scent of the man wearing the fragrance.

Jacob spoke, “I saw you enter the building. My jaw dropped at the sight of you in your dress. You look so damn sexy, especially with your red pumps.”

I smiled while he paid me well-deserved compliments. He needed to since he hadn’t called me. “I’m glad you like,” I said.

Jacob and I stayed together all night talking about our lives, current events, and our dreams. He was a cool brotha' so I gave him the digits again, this time with strict rules attached to them.

I let Jacob know I wasn't for the drama. I told him, "I don't need any females calling my phone, aiight? You should use this number because I'm not all 'willy-nilly' with the digits."

He said, "I'm not even like that beautiful. And the digits will get used."

When I went home that night, I was feeling myself a little too much. I finally got the man. All I had to do was keep the man.

My Man

Jacob and I started to become close friends. We went to different events together, such as anniversary parties, game tournaments, movie premiers, and more.

I wanted more than just a friendship, but I didn't want to push the envelope. Our connection was out of this world. I didn't want to let a good man like him slip through my fingers. Jacob and I could talk for hours about absolutely nothing. Sometimes, we looked deep into each other's eyes, pulling out something about one another that we tried to conceal.

Seeing that we were just friends, I didn't stop associating with my other male friends. Even if we did become an item, I wouldn't let my friendships blow in the wind. My male friends gave me great advice on life and helped me understand the male perspective. Matter of fact, I had some masculine qualities of my own: I didn't see anything wrong with dating someone else right after you ended a relationship, I'm not big on someone talking too much or complaining, and it's always all about me.

It was Friday night and Jacob decided to spend the weekend with me. This came as a shock to me because it was hard for him to spend any weekend with me. He owned his own marketing company and was always out of town. I requested the weekend off because I needed time off from work so I could really take on the 'All-About-Me Mentality'.

"Babe, I need you to go somewhere with me," Jacob said as if it was utterly important.

Looking suspicious, I asked, "Where?"

"I need to make a run and I want you to come along for the ride."

I didn't see what a little run could hurt. I was probably just going to stay in the house anyways. I threw on a pair of jeans, a halter top, and some flip flops.

Sun rays hit my glistening body as Jacob led me to his 2009 Yukon Denali. My body slid on his leather, right in the middle of the passenger seat. I looked at him rockin' the latest Sean John eye wear, while I wore some Baby Phat dimmers.

I sat back, relaxing to the tunes of Melanie Fiona playing on the radio. We came to a red light at 161 and Karl Road. Suddenly, Jacob peered at me. I smiled at him; however, he didn't return the smile until moments later. Weird, but ok.

Next thing I knew, we were on I-71 South going towards Cincinnati. After thirty minutes of wondering where Jacob was taking me, I finally asked him, "Where are we going?"

"It's a surprise, just relax."

After about fifteen minutes of fighting with my body to stay awake, I lost the fight to my diagnosed behavior. That's right, my friends diagnosed me as being narcoleptic. It didn't take me long to fall asleep, even though I tried my best to stay awake.

I awoke to a horizon of green grass stretched for miles and the rhythms of Robin Thicke. The clock read 5:15 pm. We left my house at 12 pm. Where the heck was this dude taking me? An overhead sign read I-75 South. My eyes surveyed Jacob trying to figure out his intent. Would this man hurt me?

I wanted to scream, but I couldn't make this man think I was afraid of him. Plus, I couldn't even formulate the words of help because my body was so exhausted that I just sat and said nothing. Was I overreacting?

Jacob took the next exit, which took us off the interstate. He turned right and made an immediate left into the gas station. Jacob stopped the car, looked at me, and began to speak.

"It's about time you woke up. I thought I had to hit you over the head with a crowbar."

My arms went straight up, and a yawn came out of my mouth. Jacob pulled me closer to him, bringing me into his lap. He touched my face with one hand, while the other hand caressed my back.

"*Tasha*, I can't hold my feelings for you any longer. I tried the friendship thing, but I can't stand for you to talk to anyone else. I really care for you and want you to be my woman."

Exactly the words I wanted to hear since we began dating; however, I had to make sure he wasn't trying to kill me on this trip.

"Jacob, where are we going?"

Jacob looked at me like a mutt that had just shitted on his Persian rug. He exhaled forcefully.

"We're going to Tennessee. I rented a suite for us to stay until Sunday."

A big smile swept across my face as I embraced him into my arms.

"Why didn't you tell me? I don't have anything to wear."

Jacob smiled. "You know I got you. Tasha. Back to my question: Will you be my woman?"

Knowing I had the upper hand, I looked at him mischievously.

"Well…" I stopped in mid-sentence and looked at him.

Jacob stared at me firmly. "Tasha, quit playing. This is serious. I really care about you."

His words were sincere. My soul began to shine so much on the inside that it showed its effects on the out.

"Yes. I'll be your woman."

The Rules of Love

Loving Jacob had been good thus far. We were going on 3 months of being together. It was strange for me at first because I was so used to being by myself. I couldn't believe some of the work that went into being in a relationship.

I thought it was cute when Jacob got jealous of me talking to other males. To me, it showed me he cared. You could practically see his veins popping out of his head when my phone rang, which was about every 5 minutes.

One night my phone rang repeatedly until I finally picked it up.

"Hello?"

"What's up, girl?"

"What's up, Joe Smo'. What you been up to?"

"Nothing much homie. I was thinking about you and wanted to check up on you."

As my conversation became longer than the five minutes intended, I could see Jacob's uneasiness as he paced the room.

"All right, see you in a few," I stated, hanging up the phone.

"J-boogie." I said as I approached Jacob. He didn't respond but kept pacing the floor. I'm not even sure if he realized that I had come closer to him.

"Jacob!" The third time his name came out somewhat stern and high pitched. Damn! He was frustrating me. Calling him like he had a damn hearing problem.

"WHAT?" He blared, looking at me with eyes that could have pierced my soul into damnation. I knew Jacob was upset, but so was I. It was evident that I had to use my KIB KIT KIM strategy: 'Keep it brief, keep it on track, and keep it moving'.

"My friend Joseph is coming over."

Jacob's eyes looked somberly into mine.

"I'm going to take a shower. I'll be back."

I returned from the shower to a dark room and a deep voice asking, "So, you doing this dude? I mean, you took a shower and shit like this ya boo."

"Nope. Joseph just wants to go out and grab a bite to eat, if that is ok with you?"

"So, he says jump and you jump? I see how you are."

What was with Jacob and his new attitude toward me? He acted like I was supposed to eat, sleep, and breathe his name. This dude had another thing coming.

The doorbell rang.

"I'll be right there!" I yelled, hopping around the room trying to put my pants and shirt on in a hurry. "Tell him I'll be right there Jacob."

When I walked in the room, there was nothing but silence. My eyes connected with Joe's as I smiled with my eyes and my body.

"Joe Smo!" I yelled with enthusiasm.

"Whudd up Taz?"

Joe placed his arms underneath my armpits and around my back. His face pressed into mine while his lips veered to the right, digging a dimple into my check. He swayed me back and forth in his arms and held me tightly.

After what seemed like hours, Joe finally put me down.

"Taz, I want you to meet Nikki." Nikki shook my hand as if I was the help at one of her mansions and she didn't want to dirty her hands with the likes of me.

"It's a pleasure," Nikki stated looking me up and down. Inwardly, I wanted to punch this girl's lights out for staring at me like I was infected with some type of communicable disease. However, I knew I had to be on my best behavior because she was Joe's girl. He had to deal with her, not me.

"That it is," I said with poise as I made my way over to Jacob and placed my arm around his.

"Joe, this is Jacob."

"What's up man?"

"Chillin," *Jacob* responded looking unenthused while providing enough nonverbal communication to state I was already taken.

"Cool. So how did you and Taz meet anyways?

Joe didn't play around when it came to wanting to know something. Could we at least act like we liked each other, eat, and then discuss it? I'm just saying.

"That's a topic for another discussion."

Really Jacob? Was it really a topic for another discussion? My boo was all hot and bothered by this dude for no good reason.

Joe looked a little perturbed, but it quickly faded.

"Well, let's go," Joe said after a while.

“I’m hungry.”

We chose to go to Bridget’s Soul Food Cooking on Mount Vernon Avenue. It was the best place in town to get some of the world’s finest Southern cuisines.

Joe and I discussed our college days and what made our friendship so amazing. He even brought up information about my past, which made Jacob comment eagerly.

“Taz, are you still a lightweight in drinking? I remember a few times you tried to hang with the big boys and we had to tuck the little pup in for the night.”

I laughed because it was true. My alcohol consumption level was low, which meant I was tipsy halfway through the first drink.

Jacob responded by saying, "She's a big girl now. She can handle whatever you throw at her."

Joe looked me in the face before responding, "Is that right?"

"Yep," Jacob responded.

Nikki and I said nothing as Joe and Jacob competed over who knew me the best. It was funny because why did men always have to compete over stupid stuff?

I thought it would be great for Jacob to meet one of my male friends so it could ease his tension when I talked to them. Jacob was acting up though and I couldn't have him acting like that toward my other friends. Matter of fact, Joe was acting up too. I could feel the aggression rising in the room.

The night ended with dinner. Joe wanted to go to the movies; however, I knew Jacob wasn't feeling him and Joe's girl wasn't feeling me. There was no need for us to put on a front for the sake of each other. It was time for the night to end before it became more unpleasant.

When Jacob and I got to my house, he was acting a bit strange. He paced through each room talking to himself.

"Jacob."

"That damn girl gonna make me have to hurt somebody," Jacob mumbled under his breath.

"Jacob," I yelled eagerly.

"What? Don't you see me thinking?"

This dude had to be mad. I mean. Yelling at me in my own damn house. Did he lose his scruples?

"Jacob. You need to get it together. You have been acting pissy ever since Joe came."

Jacob did not respond. He kept pacing and mumbling.

While lying in the bed, Jacob finally said something.

"Babe, I hate feeling jealous and I was very jealous tonight. You had me around one of your college friends who knows more about you then me. I don't like that feeling because it's like I am competing for you."

The thing about it was, I had to respect Jacob. He was honest with me, which I couldn't say for some of the men in my previous relationships. Although he was an envious nimrod, he was my envious nimrod. To be a little honest, his jealousy was a little cute. It wasn't like hit me over the head type of cute, but like aww he cares type of cute.

Jacob went on to state what else he didn't like, which seemed like Jacob's rules to love:

1. No going out with other men
2. If you weigh over 170 pounds, it's a done deal
3. I must go with you when you hang out with your friends to protect you; however, you cannot go with me and my friends
4. No meeting my female friends because that will only make you jealous, because they are very attractive
5. My money is my money and your money is my money
6. You must answer your phone or else I will call you over and over again until you do

"Oh, really?"

I began to wonder, what I had got myself into with him. This outwardly good-looking man turned into the lady from that one psychotic movie. You know the one.

The Affair

Jacob and I had been dating for a good 8 months. I really believed I was dating 'Ike'. I could hear him internally say, "*Annamae, Annamae*". All he needed was a slicked back hairdo and flashy clothing to compliment his persona.

Sometimes, Jacob received calls late at night, which made me wonder who the hell was calling my man? I started to think about his so-called rules. Fuck that, I told myself that over and over in my mind but did the direct opposite when he came around. I was like putty in his hands when he asked me to do or stop doing certain things to help our relationship.

This dude had me believing that everything was my fault and that I was the reason for the problems in our relationship.

"Oh! You didn't take out the trash, that's why we're not going out. You didn't fix my dinner, that's why I'm talking to a mysterious person late at night."

What made me upset was the fact that Jacob left the room to talk to the person on the phone or whispered very lightly. I asked him about it, but he only became upset that I would accuse him of cheating. Why was it that when you asked someone a question, they automatically assumed you were accusing them of something? If I was accusing him of something, I would say "YOU FUCKING CHEATER!" I wanted to believe him; however, something deep in my soul told me that this man could not be trusted.

Maybe my insecurities came from the way he told me about his daily activities without me asking a single word. It was like he wanted me to know he went somewhere with such and such, in case one of my friends saw him. Or the way he asked me to go places with him and at the last minute came up with an excuse why I couldn't go. There was this one time when he asked me to go to a work function with him and then at the last minute said, "I'm sorry, I forgot to buy you a ticket."

I wanted to say "The hell you mean I don't have a ticket? You best be getting me a ticket" I said nothing though. I kept my thoughts to myself.

He also only stayed the night on Tuesdays and Thursdays. It was peculiar we had to set days to spend time with each other. If he was my man, why couldn't we do that sporadic type of stuff like making love on the kitchen table? Was that too much for me to ask for?

The weekend approached quickly. It was already Saturday night and I had to work. I invited Jacob to come over, but he declined. He said he had to go out of town. How much more of this out-of-town shit could I take?

I arrived at The Flavor just in time to talk to J-E for a second. Our relationship had never been the same since J-E had come on to me and I had declined his invitation. He was also very upset that I was dating Jacob. He told me from day one that he didn't like him and there was something strange about him.

"Hey, J-E, how's it going?" He responded, "Fine," and kept working. Well, if that wasn't a good indication that fun time was over, I wasn't sure what would be one.

I responded, "That's good." I didn't want to give him an opportunity to see I was hurt by his mistreatment. Work was no longer fun. Play time was over and work became work.

I grabbed my pen and headed upstairs. Suddenly, I began to feel strange. A queasy sensation set in and wouldn't let go. I took all I could handle for about an hour and then reported to J-E.

"Hey, J."

"Taz, are you ok? You look sick."

"I don't feel good. I need to lie down for a while."

"Ok, just this one time." He looked at me, smiled, and gave me his office key. I fell asleep instantly on his couch.

J-E's door opened.

"Are you up Taz?"

I yawned and stretched my arms upward. My fingers moved over my eyes and rubbed the tired out.

"Yes, did you need help?"

He laughed and shook his head. I wondered what the laughter stemmed from,

so I checked my watch. My watch read 3:15am. The club had been closed for about 45 minutes. I also had to laugh.

"I guess it is a little too late for help, huh?"

"Yes, it is."

We both began to speak at once; however, he dominated the conversation, so I listened.

"Taz, I miss you. I miss our playfulness, the way you use to look at me. Man, what I am really trying to say is that I miss my best friend. I don't want to lose you over something this silly."

Talk about candidness. J-E was always honest, so I couldn't expect anything different when talking to him.

"J-E, I missed you too. It's been hard working here knowing that we were once good friends."

He cut me off and began talking again. I knew he really had something to say, so I paid him my undivided attention.

"Taz, I can't take back my feelings for you. There's something inside of me that wants to be with you. Something that wants to caress your skin, protect every inch of your body, and give you the world. Girl, I would give you whatever your heart desired. I can't even hate you right now because you are in a relationship, because I was in one when I approached you. Right now, I know all you can offer me is a friendship. Well, that's until ole' boy messes up. When he does, I'm going to be right there to pick up the pieces. Believe that."

J-E once again, left me speechless. I had to say something though, so I thought very hard before speaking.

"J, thanks for your honesty. That is what I love about you. You are a real person. I can always expect you to tell me the truth. I can't say that my relationship will last or that we can be together if it ends. All I can say is that you are a good friend. I respect, love, and cherish you."

We ended our conversation at 3:45 am because it was late. J-E told me to call him when I got home.

When I got home it was 4:20 am. I took the long way home and stopped by the gas station to get some gas. The first thing I did when I got home was plop straight down on the couch. I didn't feel nauseated anymore, just tired. While I sat on the sofa for a while, my phone rang.

"Hello."

"Taz, didn't I tell you to call me when you got home?"

"Sorry J-E."

"Taz, I hope you are ok. If you need anything, please call me."

"Ok, thank you."

Once I hung up the phone, I heard a strange beeping noise. It was a familiar noise, but I couldn't place my finger on it. I searched all through my house. The noise would fade and then get louder. Finally, I was heading in the right direction because the noise got louder and louder.

It was coming from underneath my bed. I leaned over my bed, while holding my hurting stomach.

Jacob's cell phone was under my bed. He never went anywhere without his cell phone. He would return hours after leaving town, just to get it. I guess that was something that I didn't understand. He had two phones and the one he left, he rarely used.

His phone kept beeping. I pushed a button to turn the beeping noise off. I happened to glance at his screen. It revealed 20 missed calls. Whoever was calling him really wanted him bad. You know me, I just had to know who had been calling my man repeatedly. I looked through his missed call list. All the calls received were stamped with the name Jessie.

"Who in the hell is Jessie?" If it was a man, why would he call him at odd hours of the night? The time stamp from each call began at 12 am and ended at 4:16 am. Jessie had called right before I got home. My mind began to wonder if this dude was trying to play me.

There were text messages from Jessie too, so I did what any normal female would do if she wanted to find out who was calling her man at odd hours of the night.

The last message from Jessie was at 4:06 am. The message read: "Hey baby, I miss you. Where are you? I thought you were going to be home this weekend. Our baby wants to see his daddy. He asked about you all day today. I have a surprise for you. Love your wife, Jessie."

"WIFE!"

How could I have been so stupid? Maybe it wasn't my entire fault because he didn't wear a wedding ring. There was something about him though that I just could not put my finger on. I should have known. Why did I always get involved with the wrong men? It was like I had a magnetic attraction for losers, want-to-be gangsters, abusers, and my latest attraction, married men. My life could not get any worse.

I felt horrible when I woke up in the morning. How could I be so low to mess with a married man?

Suddenly, my house phone rang. I didn't feel like talking so I let it ring. My stomach began to hurt again. "Oh, *GOD*. What was wrong with me? Why was my stomach hurting?"

You know what?

I couldn't remember the last time I had my menstrual cycle this month. My cycle usually came like clockwork.

On the top of my desk was a calendar. I jumped out of bed and retrieved it. I flipped through the pages frantically looking for my last dated cycle. Today was July 26, 2009. My last noted menstrual cycle was May 12, 2009.

"2 MONTHS."

I was two months behind. I started to get antsy.

"Am I pregnant?"

Jacob and I had stopped using condoms the third month of our relationship. Neither one of us had any diseases, I knew that for sure. I had that brutha' checked out the second month of us dating. Jacob didn't have anything to worry about on my end because I got checked regularly and protected myself.

What was I going to do? I wasn't married. What would my mother and father think of me? My mind began thinking about all types of things, but I was interrupted by my phone ringing. Who could be calling me repeatedly?

"Hello." I answered the phone with an attitude.

"Hey babe. How are you doing?"

JACOB. Did I really want to talk to him? My mind was saying hang up, but my heart said hold on. I was in love with Jacob and could not shake it. I began to wonder if his love was a lie.

"Tasha, are you still there?"

If I was pregnant, how would we raise a child together? He was married with a child already.

"Tasha."

"Yeah, I'm here."

"What's wrong? Why are you acting so distant?"

"Oh, just thinking about you."

"So, what are you thinking about? Are you thinking about us being together Tuesday night? About us making love? Which one?"

"Neither. I'm thinking about how you lied to me. How you made me think I was the only woman in your life. How you already had a family with a child. All that BS you fed me. How I hate your guts right now. How..."

"Tasha, what are you talking about?"

"Are you going to sit here and lie to me? Do you think I'm a fool? What would Jessie think if she knew you were with me?"

The phone conversation became quiet. I guess he was lost for words at me confronting him about his wife. After a minute or so he mustered up some words.

"Tasha, you have no right to question me about my business. Haven't I been good to you? Haven't I been a man to you? You are just like the other women I have dated; A snooping slut." His words felt so cold and hurtful.

"Spoken like a true cheater."

That was all that I could say. How could a gentleman from two days ago turn so spiteful? Where was the Jacob I met in the club?

"Well, now that I know where I stand, you can pick up your crap on Tuesday night," I said. "I'll leave them on the porch. Peace."

Once I hung up the phone, it rang back immediately. I let the answering machine pick it up this time.

"Tasha, baby. I'm so sorry. I don't know what made me say those words. Please call me back. Let's talk about this."

Oh, no thank you. He had one time to flip out on me and that was his one time. I'm like a slot machine. You can beg and plead for your money back or my love, but once it's gone, it's gone.

I threw on some jogging pants and a shirt and headed to the grocery store. I had to find out what was going on with my stomach.

My garage door opened slowly as I sped down McNaughton Road toward my home. Why did things go so slow when you were in a hurry? I pulled my car into the garage and hit the close button. My car door flew open, and I hopped out.

In running to the bathroom, I tripped over the carpet in the hallway. As I picked myself off the floor, I asked, “Why me?” Why did things like this happen to me?

I entered the bathroom with one thing on my mind. Was I pregnant? To make sure the tests were error free, I took both tests and followed the directions precisely.

Just as I finished the second test, the doorbell rang. All I could think about was hiding. I knew it had to be Jacob trying to get back into my life. It had only been an hour or so; was he that desperate?

“Taz.”

I recognized that voice from anywhere. It was Mo’. I opened the door and motioned her to come inside.

"Damn, are you having a bad day or what?" she asked.

This really wasn't a good time for me. Mo' was the type that made you want to slap her 24/6.5.

"Something like that," I replied.

"What's going on with your outfit and hair? And where have you been? I have been trying to call you all day."

"I've been hanging out."

"Ooookay. It must be that time of the month, huh? Or are you depressed because Jacob is not here?

"Negative," I replied.

"I don't see why you get all empathetic when it comes to that dude. He's just another playboy in a suit. I will never know what you see in him."

I had about all I could take from Mo'. She was my girl, but she was overstepping her boundaries. This trick was getting on my nerves.

"So, when are you going home?" My words were a bit stern and very hurtful, but true to how I was feeling now.

"Well, I missed you too bebe. If I didn't know you, I would be really offended, but I'm not. Anyways, let me get straight to the point."

I knew she wouldn't leave, so I listened.

"Didn't you say Jacob was going to be out of town this weekend?"

"Yes, I did."

"Well, I seen that negro the other night."

"Oh, did you?" I responded, wanting to know more.

"Remember when I told you I was dating this guy named Chuck?

"Yeah, you met him at Applebee's, right?"

"Yeah. Well, Chuck had a little get together the other night. Girl, you should have been there. It was cute men everywhere. You would have had a ball or a couple if you know what I mean. I wore a black velvet dress with stilettos. Girl, you should have seen me.

"Mo', get back to the story."

"Okay, I got a little caught up in what I was wearing. Anyways, the party was jumping. I happened to look up in the corner and seen Jacob. He was with this woman in a tight blue dress. She was brown skin with light brown eyes. She was slender and wore well-manicured nails."

"How do you know her whole profile?"

"Taz, come on now. What's my name? I knew if I was bringing back scoop, it had to be legit."

This was too much for me right now. I just found out *Jacob* was married with a kid, I might be pregnant, and now he was dating other people.

"So, Chuck decided to introduce me to Jacob. It was funny because I think he remembered me from the time we met at The Flavor."

"Plus, I have pictures of you and Coli all around here."

"Well, he looked and shook my hand in a strange way. All night long, he looked in my direction to see if I was looking at him. And you know what?"

"What?"

"I was. I wanted him to feel my eyes burning a hole deep into his skin."

"That's too bad."

"Too bad. Is that all you are going to say? We need to go give him a piece of our minds."

"Girl, that's not my demeanor. I am a woman; I must act like one."

"Okaaay, Ms. 'I'm every woman'. What's really going on with you? You have been acting strange ever since I walked into your house."

"I'm just tired of men. They are so manipulative. I see why I was by myself for so long."

"Is this coming from the same girl that was in love just a month ago? Ms., Jacob can't do anything wrong."

Mo' was starting to irk me again, so I had to let her have it. I had to let her know that I was the Queen Bee in this house, and she was a guest.

"Mo', you know what?"

"Girl, hold that thought. I got to use the bathroom."

Mo' went to the bathroom and closed the door. As she spent a few minutes in the restroom, I realized something, "The Pregnancy tests." Oh, my *GOD*! What was I going to do? I just knew that she would see them on the counter.

I sat in the chair frantically waiting for her to come out. The door opened slowly. Mo' held the pregnancy tests in her hand.

"Taz, what's up with this?"

My first reaction was how could she? She was so nosey. Why did she have to go through my personal business? I know it was on the counter, but what gave her that right?

"Mo', how could you? That is my business."

"Taz, just answer my question."

I looked at her trying to gather my words. My words were stuck in my throat. What could I say besides stating the facts?

The Obsession

All weekend, I laid in bed not wanting to do anything. I was still pondering on my conversation with Mo'. She wanted to know if I was pregnant, so I told her. The two pregnancy tests I took revealed that I was pregnant. This was not my weekend. I had to go to the doctor's office soon. A professional opinion would give me the information I needed.

On Sunday night, my phone rang straight for about twenty minutes. The first five rings registered Jacob's number, but the ones after that were private. It had to be Jacob trying to trick me.

The phone rang again, so I answered.

"Hello?"

"Where the hell you been? I have been trying to call you since yesterday. Do you think I have time to waste calling you all the damn time?"

Jacob really started to show a change in his character. This was something I hadn't seen in him, except this one time. One time he called me on the phone and told me he wanted me to fix him dinner if I had time. My day was hectic, so I didn't have time to make dinner. When Jacob came over, he was really sweet and nice. Well, that was until he found out that there was no dinner.

That man did a complete 180. He mumbled something under his breath and cut his eyes at me. My first thought was, no this dude wasn't catching an attitude with me and giving me the side eye. I gave him a look, which meant that I wasn't having it. I think that was when he realized that I wasn't the type of woman he could pushover.

"Tasha, do you hear me talking to you?"

Jacobs's words started to push through my past thoughts of his first disrespectful words to me.

"Jacob, who do you think you are talking to like that? I'm not someone who will sit here and take your ridicule. When you decide to talk to me like a person, call me back."

I hung up the phone. What was I going to do about the baby? I didn't want to have a baby because I wasn't financially where I wanted to be. I could give the baby up for adoption once I had it. The thought quickly faded because if I went through nine months of carrying the baby, I would want to keep the kid.

The next call registered a Mr. Jay Evans.

"Hello."

"Hey, Baby Girl. Just checking in on you. How are you doing?"

"I have been stressing a lot lately. I think I need to get out."

"Well, that's why I'm calling. I have two premiere tickets to go to see a new movie. Do you want to go?"

"I could use a night out on the town with one of Columbus's finest. What time should I be ready?"

"It starts at 9:30 pm. Be ready by 8:45pm."

I needed to get out of the house and rectify my relationship with J-E. Although he apologized the other night, it wasn't the same.

J-E was my buddy. We used to do a lot together before I got with Jacob.

I had to make sure my outfit to the movies was stylish. The whole intention was to look enticing and off-limits at the same time.

A little before J-E was supposed to show up, the doorbell rang. I answered the door, only to be surprised by the person on the other side. It was Jacob. How was I going to get rid of him?

"Hey baby. I've missed you so much."

Jacob spoke to me like our fight had never happened. Something was seriously wrong with him, and I was beginning to figure it all out.

"Jacob, what are you doing here? I thought you were working?"

"I wanted to spend time with my baby, so I thought I would pay you a special surprise."

I responded, "Surprise yes. Special no."

Jacob looked as if someone had slapped him right in his face. Before Jacob could respond to anything, I cut him off.

"You must go. I'm leaving."

Jacob responded, "Where are you going?" in a very powerful voice.

"Out. That's all you need to know."

Tension began to rise between Jacob and me when the doorbell rang. Oh, no. What was I going to do? I just knew Jacob would be pissed.

Jacob looked me in my eyes right before I walked over to answer the door.

"Hey, baby girl. Are you ready?"

"One minute. Jacob is here. He was just leaving."

Jacob came into the living room and looked J-E up and down.

I said to Jacob, "Leaving, right? You can pick up your things on Tuesday."

Jacob's eyes moved from J-E to me. Right before Jacob exited the door, he glanced back. He gave me a long stare that sent chills down my spine.

Where You Go, I Go

Tonight, was going to be the best night ever. J-E and I were going on a date. It was the best way for me to stop thinking about all my troubles with Jacob.

"So, Ms. Lady, what's been going on with you?"

"Too much to tell you in one sitting. Let's just enjoy this time."

"Ok."

J-E looked at me with concern. I think he could tell something was going on with me. I usually spilt my guts out to J-E; however not now. I had to watch what I said to J-E because I knew he had feelings for me.

"Ms. Taz, are you ready?"

"Yes, sir. Let me grab my purse."

J-E and I walked down the sidewalk close to each other as we headed toward his car. He drove a black BMW with black tinted windows. His car had to be a 2008. J-E walked over to the passenger side of the car and opened it.

"Ladies first," he said as he smiled at me. J-E was very gentle and caring. From day one, he had always been gentle towards me. Inside, I knew that he liked me. He treated me differently then he treated everyone else. He let me get away with things he wouldn't let others get away with, not even his family. I knew tonight would be hard for me. I liked J-E, but I didn't want him to be a part of the situation with Jacob.

We drove down Olentangy River Road in silence for about 10 minutes. I didn't know what to say to J-E.

"Tasha."

"Yes?" I spoke. What was he about to ask me? He hadn't called me Tasha since.... Well, I couldn't remember a time when he did.

"Are you happy?"

"Happy with what? Our friendship? My life?

"With Jacob?"

Man, I didn't expect this conversation for a while. I guess it was time for me to stop holding my cards so close to my chest and reveal my hand.

"No. He's not the man I thought he was. I thought I was getting a filet mignon meal, instead I got a box of Lucky Charms. No comparison."

J-E burst out laughing. I hadn't heard him laugh for quite some time. I joined in with his laughter because it was funny, at least the comparison part.

"See, I miss that."

"What?" I replied.

"I miss you and your funny comments. I miss us hanging out together. I miss you nudging me at work, stroking my face, and flirting at work."

Dang! Was I all of that to J-E? This dude really missed me huh. Well, who wouldn't miss me thought. I was sexy, confident, and every man's dream. He had a right to miss me. Ok, enough of my narcissism, although it was very hard. Ha!

“Well, I guess I missed you,” I said with a smile. He smiled back.

We approached the movie complex, where our movie would take place. As we pulled into the parking lot a strange feeling came over me. I felt someone had been following us. I didn’t want to make nothing into something, so I didn’t say anything. Maybe with all the Jacob drama, I had a touch of paranoia going on. Was I becoming paranoid?

J-E was such a gentleman the whole night. He assisted me to my seat, got me popcorn and water, and was what I needed for the night.

As we walked toward the main entrance, I caught a glimpse of someone that looked just like Jacob. He wore the same outfit and had the same build.

“That couldn’t be.”

“What’s wrong?” J-E replied.

“Is that Jacob over there looking at us?”

J-E turned around and saw Jacob staring at both of us. Jacob looked lost, confused, and malicious all at the same time.

“Yes. Did he follow us?”

“I have no clue,” I responded. I began to think about the car that followed us to the movies. Could that have been Jacob? Ok, he was really starting to scare me. He was scaring me to the point that I did not want to stay home alone.

Jacob moved closer to us and spoke. “Fancy meeting you here.” His words were very nonchalant compared to earlier.

We stood motionless and did not respond for a few seconds.

“Well, are you both just going to stand there and say nothing?”

“Oh, yeah,” I replied.

“Right,” J-E added.

We didn’t know what to say. Jacob finally exhaled forcefully and left our presence. He moved hurriedly toward the exit, mumbling under his breath.

“Are you ok?” J-E said concernedly.

“I don’t know. I think he followed us from my house. I saw a car following us.”

“You know what? I did too.”

The next question J-E asked was, “Are you going to be ok home alone?”

“I’m not sure because he sort of freaked me out.”

“Well, I’m not being forward or anything, but you can come and stay with me for the night. That’s only if you want to stay.

Should I stay with J-E or go home? It was hard because I knew J-E had some strong feelings for me. I didn’t want to put myself out there where J-E thought we were an item. The other hard decision was that I did not want to be home alone. Was Jacob capable of hurting me?

“Ok,” I replied.

“Ok?”

“Ok, I will stay the night with you tonight.”

J-E asked me if I needed to stop anywhere to pick up some extra clothing because he did not want to take me home. He did not want Jacob following us to his house.

"Yes, can we go to Mack's?" Mack's was the only place I could think of that was open 24 hours.

On our way to J-E's house, the ride was very quiet. We were finally spending the night with each other because of unnecessary circumstances.

This would be the very first time that I had been in J-E's home. He had invited me over for parties and social gatherings, but I had always declined his offers.

"Home sweet home," J-E said as we pulled up to a nice white condo. The condo looked very nice on the outside. It had a garage big enough to fit three cars in it. Ok, maybe I was exaggerating just a little bit, but it was close.

Wow. His home was immaculate. He had cream marble flooring in the kitchen. His kitchenware looked as though it had never been used. His kitchen colors were silver and black with a hint of red.

Next was his living room, which was beautiful. He had a fish tank in the middle of his wall, which separated the kitchen from the living room. The beautiful blue and orange fish mixed colors with the decor of his kitchen. His couch was blue, which set off his cream carpeting. A picture of an elegant black woman dancing gracefully adorned his wall. The woman was dressed in a blue and green sheer skirt with a light blue body hugger.

He gave me a tour of his home. I was amazed at J-E's house. It was evident that he took pride in his house and himself. Was this just what I needed in my life? Thoughts of us being together filled my head; however, I had to let them go. I had to think about how to get rid of Jacob first before I could move on.

"So, Ms. Smith," *Jacob* said so *smoothly*. "Would you like something to drink?"

"Sure," I replied, not knowing what to expect.

Jacob went to the cupboard and took out two wine glasses. He returned with some white zinfandel. Then he asked, "Is this fine?"

"Yes," I answered with sheer sexiness. It was my time to put the bad times behind me and move toward the future. I needed to relax and focus on me for once. J-E would be just the person to help me focus on me. He was so sincere and compassionate.

I decided to run to the bathroom and freshen up. I stood in the bathroom mirror, then took a deep breath in and exhaled out. This was the first time in months I had been stress free. I wanted to enjoy it. I needed to enjoy it. After I freshened up, I made my way back to the living room with J-E.

J-E knew exactly what he was doing. He turned on music." The lights were dimmed, and strawberries were placed on the table.

Damn, I said internally. This boy was on his p's and q's. He knew what it took to make a woman lose control. This girl right here though was not losing control.

"Don't lose control girl," I told myself.

I sipped my wine, carefully watching J-E's every move. He watched me watching him. A devious smile graced his face as he took a sip of his wine. This was a set up. J-E had set this whole thing up. I had to admit it though, if this was my first date with J-E, he could have whatever he was planning on getting tonight. He could have it all. Since it wasn't our first encounter I had to hold out. Do like *Madea* says and clank, clank.

"Tasha, why don't you come a little closer? I promise I won't bite too hard." His voice trailed off on the too hard part.

My eyes examined J-E's body position, the way he licked his lips and how his right index finger circled the opening of his wine glass.

Tasha don't give in girl. You can do it. The pep talks helped somewhat. However, I could feel myself wanting J-E more and more as he spoke. J-E knew I wanted him, I just knew it.

I diverted my attention from J-E to the fish tank. My movement toward the fish was slow and sexy because I knew he was watching. I gazed at the fish and watched them swim for about fifteen seconds. Then J-E walked up behind me and placed his arms around me.

"Shhhh," he said as he pulled me close to him. His grasp was powerful and protective. His lips moved up and down my neck. A feeling of desire ran through my head as his hands moved from my stomach to my hips.

Without further ado, J-E turned me around so quickly that I did not have time to react. He enclosed my lips within his. A pleasant tingly feeling surged from my neck to the portions of my back he caressed, and finally to my toes. I could not turn the feeling off no matter how bad I tried.

Our lips moved together, taking a piece of each other as each kiss came one after the other. J-E positioned his hands below my underarms and lifted me straight off the floor. I was aroused even more by him picking me up.

He made a fantasy of mine turn into reality. I moaned as he positioned my legs around his waist.

Our connection was not disturbed for one moment. We kept kissing like we were newlyweds, and he was going off to war.

J-E moved swiftly with me in his arms. Next thing I knew, we were on silk sheets. The room was dark, so I couldn't see anything. I moaned as his hands moved from my legs to my stomach, to my chest, then finally to the spot that sent me into convulsions; my back. My back was the most sensitive portion of my body and I moaned powerfully with every single touch.

"Baby, I want you to be mine."

J-E's words really sent my body into a frenzy. "Tasha, baby."

"Yes?" I responded

"Will you be mine, Tasha?"

I replied, knowing the extent of my words, but also living in the moment, "Yes".

We become one that night.

In the morning, I woke up before J-E. I fixed him some pancakes, eggs, and some turkey bacon with some orange juice. His plate was made and set on the table. Next to his plate I wrote him a note which read:

Dear J-E,

Thank you for last night. We connected on a whole new level that I had never imagined. I needed to clear my head, so I left. Call me later this week, please.

-Tasha

I know, what a way to wake up? A missing girl and a Dear John letter. I needed time to absorb what had taken place last night. I wanted it to happen; however, it seemed a little premature.

I left J-E's house with a new problem to deal with. How would our friendship continue after this?

The Visit

"Ms. Smith, the doctor will see you now."

It was a question in the back of my mind that I could not get past. Was I pregnant?

"Hello Dr. Evans, how are you doing?"

"I am doing great, Ms. Smith. I would ask you the same; however, I know something is wrong. You had your check up a couple of months ago and you usually don't make unscheduled visits to my office. So, what's going on?"

"I think I'm pregnant."

"Oh, really?"

"Yes! Can you tell me if I am."

"Ok. I can give you pregnancy test. Just come back around 3pm so I can give you the results."

"Why so late?"

"Because I have a busy day and I want to be able to sit down with you and talk about the results. If that is ok with you?"

"Of course. I will be back at 3 pm."

I was nervous after the test was done. My mind began to wonder about how my life would have to change drastically because the new addition. I was used to clubbing when I wanted to, going out of town on a regular basis, and just enjoying life.

Life would be so much different with a child. I could not go clubbing, well not as much. My, me-time would be very limited. I would have to make a big adjustment that I wasn't sure that I was ready to make.

How could I? me? Take on a charge like that? I was only one person, and I knew that I wouldn't want to be with Jacob. For one, he was married and two he was crazy as they came. I couldn't raise a child with a man that I couldn't trust.

I left Dr. Evan's office, glancing down at my watch on my wrist. It read 10 am on the dot. What would I do for nearly five hours? Shopping always helped me to relax, so that's what I did. Shopping had done a great job of getting my mind off my troubles. My stress was relieved momentarily. I had to stay positive and accept everything I was given at the doctor's office. I knew there was a great chance of me being pregnant. I needed to accept the results regardless of the decision I made.

I arrived at Dr. Evan's office at 3:15 pm. Traffic was backed up on 270 south. When I got into the office, the receptionist told me, "Head back to room four and Dr. Evans will be with you shortly."

I walked back to the room where I sat fidgeting with my clothing. The results of the test would make or break me. I knew I had to hold it together regardless of the results.

Dr. Evans walked straight through the door expressionless. I watched him carefully as he walked over to his stool and sat down. I tried to grasp the results through his nonverbal communication, but I just could not.

I spoke to him candidly. "Give it to me straight doc. Am I pregnant?"

"Ms. Smith, how was your day? What did you do to relieve yourself of your thoughts of being pregnant?"

It was evident this man was going to make it very hard for me. I really did not want to talk about what I had done today. I wanted the results and fast. Did he have no remorse for my condition? I wasn't paying Dr. Evans to talk about my day. I was paying him to tell me the results.

"Dr. Evans." I said his name very sharply so he would understand my position in the situation.

He responded, "Ok, I just want you to relax before I give you the results."

He gave me a look which said, I still want to know what you did.

"I shopped, ate, and now I'm here waiting for you to give me the results. So, without further ado, please."

"Ok, here it goes. Ms. Tasha Marie Smith, you are."

"I'm what? What am I?" I was very unsettled by his delay of the results.

"You are not pregnant."

"Huh, are you sure? Both tests I took indicated that I was pregnant."

"Well, pregnancy tests are only about 80 to 90% accurate. There is a 10 to 20% chance that they are incorrect."

"How could this be? I did the test twice."

"Like I mentioned before, tests can be wrong. Sometimes stress and changes in your body can cause you to miss your period. Exercising too much can also lead to changes in your period. Are you sad you're not pregnant?"

"Oh, no. More like relieved. I just don't want any unexpected surprises."

"Ok, I can understand that" the doctor said as he looked over the results further.

"How is everything else going in your life: love, work, family, everything?"

I responded, "Everything is great except for the love part. Recently, I had become a victim of a fatal attraction. The guy that I thought I loved is now stalking me. What are the chances of that happening?"

"He's stalking you? Have you gone to the police about him to get a restraining order?"

"No. I just haven't had the chance to do so."

"That is something that you cannot hold off doing. You need to go to the police station today and get a restraining order."

I told Dr. Evans that I would. If I put up a fuss with him, he would just keep on talking to me like I was one of his daughters.

"Thank you for the discussion, Dr. Evans, I really appreciate it. I must make a few runs before I head home. Thank you again."

"Sure, anything for a loyal patient," he replied with a smile.

I was so overwhelmed by the news that I almost fainted in the hallway. The news was unbelievable. This was when I knew that it would be a great day. Ms. Tasha Marie Smith would be ok.

Dead *Wrong*

It had been weeks since I last saw or heard from Jacob. The absence of Jacob was good for me because it allowed me to deal with my emotions. I knew Jacob was bad for me. He was someone who was controlling. He needed someone or something that he could control. Well, I had news for him, I was neither of the above.

I rolled out of bed, instantly deciding that I would go for a run in the park. Running would help me clear my mind from thinking about Jacob so much. I could also get a well-deserved workout. It was truly needed. Ten pounds was the amount I gained while being in a relationship. I needed to lose the extra baggage. Oh, yea, I wanted to lose weight too.

It was going to be a beautiful day. The weatherman said that it would be around 80 degrees, sunshine with a clear sky. Thinking about the beautiful day ahead made me less stressed. It was only 8 am; however, I knew I needed to get an early start to get everything finished.

I decided to take a nice long shower before I went running. I know, who in their right mind would take a shower before running? Me, that's who. I just felt so icky. I needed something to relax and refresh me. I turned on the shower to a lukewarm temperature. The water ran for a few moments before I jumped into it.

Afterwards, I walked into my bedroom covered in a towel and looked at myself in the mirror. I began to wonder how a woman so beautiful and intelligent could have gotten involved with a man so vindictive. He was so sweet and endearing in the beginning.

I was happy to get back into my routine of running; it had been way too long. Lately, I hadn't run as much because I thought I was knocked up. I didn't want to jeopardize the baby's health because of my exercise routine. The stress of being pregnant by Jacob rolled right off my shoulders. I knew that not being pregnant was my sign to leave him alone for good and find someone who wasn't controlling. In other words, I needed to find someone who was not Jacob.

I decided that I would not use my car to go jogging because the park was approximately six blocks from my home. I could get some good exercising in if I jogged. My jog started out light and brisk. It felt good to breathe in the fresh air. Every inhale relaxed my mind and eased my muscles. Every exhale gave me hope that I would make it through another day.

The park was very beautiful. Surveying the scene became a ritual of mine since J-E and I saw Jacob at the movies. I smiled at a nice couple, watched birds flying, and raced a little girl who looked as though she was 7 years old. My day could not get any better. I got to my last leg of the 2-mile trail and that was when I saw him. It was Jacob. What the hell was he doing out so early and running? He never ran with me when we were together. He didn't even like to run.

I decided to smile at him while keeping to my exercise plan. I thought if I didn't pay him any mind that he would go about his business. I was extremely wrong.

"Hey, Tasha. Can I join you?"

I was lost for words. What should I say? He was seriously stalking me. I knew my answer could send him over the top of continuing to stalk me or doing something to hurt me. My actions were very nonchalant because I knew what a stalker could do. My mother's stalker had given me proof to what stalkers were capable of doing.

When I was 15 years old, my mother committed infidelity with this guy at St. Charles Hospital, where she worked. This event changed our life traumatically. The man my mother was cheating with was very much in love with her. He would show up over our house unannounced and send her flowers and letters saying that he could not live without her.

I remember this one time when we went to the grocery store, he had followed us there. This man grabbed my mother's arm as we looked through the produce section for some fruits and vegetables. My mother told him to let her arm go, but he would not. He told her that he loved her and asked her how could she do something like that to him? He told her that he would do anything for her and that I should have been his child.

This man was very obsessed with my mother and would not let her go. My mother had to finally get a restraining order for this man.

This was the same man that years later killed himself and his previous girlfriend because she broke up with him.

I knew second hand what a stalker could do and I didn't want to be a victim or a homicide case.

"Tasha, did you hear me?" Jacob asked. I had zoned out for a minute, thinking about my mother and what she did to get rid of her stalker.

"Tasha."

"Yes?" I replied with an uninterested look on my face. I had to make it seem as if my feelings for him were over and that I had moved on.

"Can I join you in running?"

"No, I don't think that would be the best possible thing at this moment. I really need some alone time."

"Oh."

"Well, peace out." I headed straight for the parking lot. I kept looking forward as if not to seem afraid of him. I know that if I acted scare, he would play on your emotions.

I searched frantically for my car in the parking lot. Then I remembered that I didn't drive. Suddenly, my cell phone rang. It was J-E.

I felt a light touch on my shoulders as I answered the phone.

"Hello."

As I turned to respond to the light touch, I saw a large item coming toward my head. It was too late for me to duck because I wasn't anticipating the attack. It impacted and my body toppled to the ground.

"*Tasha*, wake up."

I heard a familiar voice tell me to wake up, but I couldn't seem to open my eyes. Was I dreaming? It felt like one of those days when you try to wake yourself up or get up and can't. Next, I felt something very hot touch my body, which made me flinch.

One of my eyes jerked open. The other eye would not open. I had a splitting headache that wouldn't go away. What was going on? Where was I? Who was I with? All types of questions flooded my mind, which made my head hurt even more.

I heard the laughter of a man very close.

"You know you did this to yourself, right?" He asked in a condescending voice. What had I done? Most importantly, who was this man?

"I loved you. I cared for you. I would have done anything for you. You stupid trick." His words got cold and bitter as he spoke.

"I would have given you the world, but you had to mess that up. You made me do this to you. How could you? I loved you. You stupid heifer. You make me sick. You must pay now."

My vision became clear as he approached me. It was Jacob. The last thing I remember was something hitting me across my face. My right hand moved across my face very slowly, assessing every inch. My fingers stopped over my right eye, which still would not open. It felt swollen. My eye was saturated with some type of thick substance. I saw blood as I pulled my fingers back from my eye. Was the blood from me? I tried moving my left hand; however, it was tied down to a pipe. The place in which I was held captive was cold and dreary. There was very little light that came from one light bulb in the middle of the room.

Pain within my body started to slowly distribute throughout my upper and lower extremities; however, I think most of it was flowing to my right eye. I was scared out of my mind. I didn't know what to do, or what to say. If I managed to escape, I didn't know where I would go. I didn't even know where he was keeping me.

Jacob began to speak again, this time more angrily than before. "You are dead wrong

Tasha. Dead wrong. I am going to make you pay for everything you have done to me. Consider yourself dead as of this moment forward. You are nothing to me. If I can't have you, then no one can. You must pay for what you have done. And believe me, you will pay."

He knelt beside me with a sharp knife in his right hand, while stroking it with his left hand. The nerve of this guy. This psychotic jerk. I knew I couldn't take him by myself. I had to fight crazy with crazy. It wasn't going to be easy; however, I was willing to fight for my life. It was all I could do.

My left eye surveyed the room for possible escapes and weapons. Suddenly, a drowsy feeling came over me. My left eye strained to stay open; however, there was no use. It closed slowly and I drifted off to sleep.

When I awoke, I was still on the floor tied up with rope. This time, both of my hands were tied up. My left eye surveyed the room again to locate Jacob. He was nowhere in sight.

I decided to try and escape. In my mother placing me in Girl Scouts, I learned how to tie and untie knots. Getting loose would be easy. The hard part would be escaping with one eye. I moved the rope back and forth between my hands. This effort went on for what seemed like hours. Finally, I loosened up the knots. First, I slipped my right hand through the rope and then my left.

In one quick motion, I jumped up and grabbed a couple of pens that I saw lying on the table. They were the best weapons I could find. I then ran into the bathroom and looked at my face. My eye looked extremely horrible. There was blood and pus all around my eye. It had turned black and blue from the impact of Jacob's swing. I was unrecognizable.

A sound like a garage door opening and a car pulling into the garage was heard. I just knew it was Jacob. I wanted everything to seem normal, so I resumed my place on the floor. I took the ropes and made it look like they were still tied together. I kept my eye open for the ultimate element of surprise when I attacked him.

The basement door opened. Jacob came down the steps abruptly. He glanced over at me as he headed in another direction. When he saw my eye opened, he stopped dead in his tracks.

"Hey, baby. You are looking good tonight. How about a kiss for Big Daddy." He made his way over to me and knelt on the floor. As he leaned over to give me a kiss, I grabbed his face and jabbed the side of his face forcefully with the two pens.

Jacob let out a big yell, "YOU STUPID BITCH."

He jumped up and ran around the room like I had just chopped off his penis. This was my chance to make my escape. I sprinted toward the top of the steps, only to find that the basement door had a pad lock on it.

"Dumb broad. Did you really think that it would be that easy? I told you… nobody can have you."

Jacob pulled a butcher knife from his black army vest. He looked like he was ready to go to war with his black skully on his head and dark paint underneath his eyes.

"Jacob!" I yelled at the top of my lungs. "What the hell do you want from me, you psychotic bastard?"

He looked at me as if I already knew, then he spoke the words with ease, "Your life. All I want from you is your life."

I began to cry and said to him very powerfully, "YOU CAN'T HAVE MY LIFE." My tears flowed now as Jacob made his way up the steps. I jumped through the gap between the openings in the handrail.

He jumped down the steps right behind me. Jacob grabbed my arm and sliced me straight across my back.

My shoulder blades moved inward toward my back, as I fell immediately. My body cringed in the fetal position. I tried to recover; however, could not before the next slice came. I felt the knife graze me across my left shoulder, making me grasp in agony. The pain was too much to bear.

"I told you; you were mine. I'm not gonna let no J-E, or anyone else for that matter, have you."

As his words trialed off, both of his hands went up and came down, piercing my waist with the knife.

I was a goner for sure. I knew my life had ended at the point where the knife pierced through my side and I could feel no more. Jacob then headed upstairs and unlocked the pad lock. He was gone a while, so I knew he was preparing his burial materials.

It was time to escape. I got up slowly and staggering. I let out a deep sigh, hoping that the next breath I inhaled would replenish my energy. Nothing happened. My breathing increased as I crept up the steps, hoping not to make a sound. When I reached the top of the steps, I heard a noise. It was from the upper level.

I saw a set of keys and a cell phone on the counter. I grabbed both and headed for the garage. My hand pressed my left side trying to stop the blood from oozing out. One step at a time, I told myself, trying to keep a steady stride.

I entered the garage not knowing what to expect. Rope, a machete, a shovel, and plastic bags laid upon the floor. In the corner, there was bleach and kerosene. This man had plans on killing me, and not a gunshot wound to the head type of murder. He was going to dismember me and burn me alive.

Before I lifted the garage door, I opened the car door and made sure the keys were in the ignition. I pressed the garage door opener and hoppled over to the car and shut it. My foot pressed hard against the brakes, as I quickly shifted into reverse. The garage door from the house flew open and *Jacob* came running out. The car screeched as I hit the breaks in a quick manner to change the direction of the car.

Jacob was almost crushed by the car as it swerved out of control. My vigor was slowly decreasing, making it harder and harder for me to function.

I pushed through somehow to at least drive for 20 minutes, then called 911 with my cell phone. I struggled trying to talk to the operator, drive, and hold my throbbing left side.

The car was going about 15 miles per hour on the highway with no sense of direction. A few times, I almost sideswiped a passing car. A local police officer pulled me over.

"License and registration."

My head slumped down, as I began wheezing.

“Ma’am. Ma’am. Are you ok?”

He called for backup and an emergency squad immediately. The next thing I remember was waking up and being in a hospital room.

I Choose Life

I choose life. I choose to explore the depths of the world to see what it has to offer. Travel to the most exotic but exquisite places. Taste the uniqueness of foreign cuisines and delightful winery.

I want to run rampant amongst the young and release my inner youth. Dive into the bluest sea and lavish in my achievements. Eat chocolate by the yard and indulge at my thick figure.

I want to be a woman that has been released from a harmful yet lesson-oriented relationship. I want to teach others what love is and how it should be. I want to be the type of person that I know is inside of me. It was a little late for that though. Like the saying goes “You wait long, you wait wrong.”

My life had been taken away from me in a blink of an eye. I only had two people to blame for that: Jacob and myself. Jacob’s jealousy drove him crazy. I felt every inch of the knife enter my stomach and that was the last scene that I saw.

I heard voices clear as day; however, no faces to match the voices. It was pitch-dark where I was, and I didn’t like it one bit. I tried and tried to open my eyes; however, nothing happened. My mother's voice was a constant voice that I heard. She would cradle beside me praying to GOD for my deliverance.

Why was she praying for GOD to deliver me? What was wrong?

Finally, after what seemed like forever, I awakened. I was unable to speak. Unable to yell at myself for being so stupid for loving Jacob. The last words I heard were my doctor's.

"I don't know if she will pull through. She has already lost an enormous amount of blood. Her body is working in overdrive trying to fight for her life."

A beeping sound fades and so does my life.

"Why?" I wanted to do so much with my life, now look at me. Lifeless because love consumed my life. What a sickening curse.

I grasped for air, breathing deeply. It became harder and harder for me to breathe. I wanted to hang on to life; however, didn't think I could for much longer. My life was fading from existence. My beautiful life. What was I to do?

My respirator began to work in overdrive time trying to pump fresh air into my lungs. My mother jumped up from her position and ran out of the room. She came back with the nurses. My mother fought with the nurses as she wanted to stay with me.

The nurses pushed my mother on the other side of the door and closed the blinds. Doctors and nurses came in and out of my room swiftly with a defibrillator.

I fought and fought for my life; however, this was a fight I could not win. I took in one last breath, which felt like trying to come up for air from a pool that was enclosed in glass.

The medical staff tried their best to shock life back into my body. Nothing moved within me, besides the currents from the shock. Life was gone. Nothing left in my body to fight for because Jacob had won. His wickedness consumed my body and sent me to my final resting place.

If I knew then what I know now, I would have done a lot of things differently. First, I would not have talked to Jacob. I would have hooked up with J-E and lived happily ever after. It was too late for my should of, could of, and would ofs. I was eternally paying for my decisions. Why? Why me? How was I to know that Jacob was a special case?

This was my life lesson. Though I cannot fix the decisions I made or do things differently in other relationships, I pass the torch to you. I challenge you to identify harmful relationships, look for a way out, advocate for yourself, and seek help if needed. Many women and even men are victims of detrimental relationships that sometimes claim their lives. Physical and mental violence can hinder a person's growth and development. Violence can leave mental and physical scars, which may be hard to rid due to the extinct. Get help while there is still a chance. Visit your local health department for domestic violence information, or other local agencies. Don't be a statistic; get help.

Discussion Questions

- What is the main character's name?
- What city is the main character from?
- Is Jacob and J-E the same person?
- Why does Tasha decide to work for The Flavor?
- How would you describe the characters Mo, Coli, Tasha, J-E, and Jacob?
- What does Tasha's dream in the beginning symbolize?
- Where there signs in the beginning that made you question Jacob's character?
- How would you recognize someone with aggressive behavior?

- If you witnessed a domestic violence dispute, would you help?
- Name two reasons why you should help?
- Name two reasons why you may think twice about helping someone?
- If you suspect a friend is involved in a domestic dispute, how would help them?
- Name a Domestic Violence Center in your area that you can get help or help someone else seek help?

About the author

Melica was born in a one parent household on the Southeast side of Columbus, Ohio. Being the youngest was not always easy and she had to continuously show precision with hard work and dedication.

Writing has always been an essential part of Melica's life. It helped her creatively express certain things in her life, as well as the lives of others. Melica continues to produce material that is close to her heart and that will make a difference in the lives of others. Keep an eye out for more material from her in the form of poetry, children's books, and much more.

Dead Wrong was brought to you by the
creative talents of
Melica Niccole

Look out for other titles by Melica
Such as:

Sisters of the Shield

Poetic Outlets

My Poetic Soul Unleashed

&

All in Together Girls

Melica Niccole can be contacted at
P.O. Box 29001
Columbus, Ohio 43229

www.MelicaNiccole.com

www.ingramcontent.com/pod-product-compliance
Lightning Source LLC
Chambersburg PA
CBHW030338310726
48979CB00001B/83
9798986665535